FAREWELL,
MY ORANGE

Iwaki Kei

FAREWELL, MY ORANGE

*Translated from the Japanese
by Meredith McKinney*

Europa
editions

Europa Editions
214 West 29th Street
New York, N.Y. 10001
www.europaeditions.com
info@europaeditions.com

Copyright © 2013 Kei Iwaki All Rights Reserved
First published in Japan in 2013 by Chikumashobo Ltd., Tokyo.
Publication rights for this English edition
arranged through Kodansha Ltd., Tokyo
First Publication 2018 by Europa Editions

Translation by Meredith McKinney
Original title: *Sayōnara, Orenji*
Translation copyright © 2018 by Europa Editions

Library of Congress Cataloging in Publication Data is available
ISBN 978-1-60945-478-4

Iwaki, Kei
Farewell, My Orange

Book design by Emanuele Ragnisco
www.mekkanografici.com

Cover illustration by Masaki Shiota

Prepress by Grafica Punto Print – Rome

Printed in the USA

FAREWELL,
MY ORANGE

Salimah's work began before daybreak, and around noon she went home. Once back, she tore off her clothes and stepped straight into the shower. This habit had begun on her first day of work, though the luxury of washing in all this hot water and so early in the day made her angry with herself.

Often, she cried as she showered. She twisted the two taps, the one with the blue circle and the one with the red circle, in a single movement, then stood stock-still under the water that spurted from the lotus-shaped shower head. At that moment when the cold and hot water blended to create the perfect temperature, the tears always came. She could feel their special warmth despite the hot water streaming over her.

Salimah's hair was so curly that a comb could barely get through it. It huddled almost timidly above her earlobes, and the water drops shattered off it at crazy angles. But her black skin was sleek and glossy as fine tanned leather; the suds slid smoothly down the slopes of her shoulders in delicate white stripes. Though her body had borne two children, it had none of the usual excess. The curves were clean as an egg's, with a tension that repulsed everything that might touch them. She was proud of her body, and as she washed and caressed it she wept hard.

Every soap bubble held a sob, which echoed softly against the bathroom ceiling as it burst. Sob after sob resounded there, till at last their accumulated sounds came drifting back down with the pounding water to wrap her body like white feathers. There among the clouds of steam, Salimah's voice rose to a wail.

She had been employed on the spot at the job interview a few days earlier, and told to come back the next morning at 3 A.M. wearing the garment she was handed, together with her contract. Once home, she spread out the folded square of white cloth and found a capacious knee-length work coat that opened down the front. There were dull brown stains around the cuffs and in the stomach area. Next morning, she wore it to work, and as she laboured, the big brown stains became blotted out by fresh red ones in exactly the same places.

It was now some time since Salimah had fled to this country. Even when her husband had pointed to some place on a world map and told her that was where they were going, she didn't know what her own country looked like so she couldn't really tell whether this country was close to her own or far away on the other side of the ocean. All she understood was that the place seemed to be a large island.

It could only be called complete chance that had landed them in this new home without so much as a moment to pause and take it in. Back there, people had been battling and slaughtering each other; here, an unknown landscape stretched before her. Everyone she saw was going about their normal life in peace and speaking an unrecognizable language. Salimah and her family followed the government's directives for refugees. When they were told that they were being offered a safe place to live, they could only believe that it was indeed the best choice. Their priority had been to stay alive, after all. But if they had found themselves settled in some racial melting pot, she would not now be suffering so much from her different language and skin colour. Once the grind of this new daily life had set in, like the drudgery of assembly-line work, she became aware of an enormous weight that pressed heavily on her.

In the beginning, walking near the house or out shopping, she'd felt crippled by the entangling web of strange stares from those around her. At such times, she would pretend not to notice, and simply gaze back at the staring people before her. It was impossible, or anyway impossible for her, to avert her eyes. The children gaped as they darted about her. Middle-aged women smiled uncomfortably when she met their gaze. Again and again she told herself that there must be people here who would befriend her as warmly as the people in the immigration office had. But nonetheless the weight that oppressed her heart refused to lift.

And it was hard, too, to see how her two sons, always so frisky and high-spirited, were now drooping like withered ears of wheat. They couldn't adjust to school, and were frequently left stranded on their own by the other children. Some of the naughtier children picked on them until they cried. The primary school had gone out of its way to welcome the two, and the kindhearted teachers spent their time frantically trying to protect them, but it was like trying to protect two vulnerable little doves from a circling flock of crows.

And then there was the pressing problem of language.

Since starting work she had picked up the bare minimum of words, but those were still very far from being much help in everyday life. She couldn't get hold of things she really needed. She couldn't protect her sons. And the people she came in contact with retreated as soon as they realised that she didn't understand what they said.

So she did everything in fear and trepidation, and the same was true for her husband and sons. Even the sudden loud cry of a passing bird made them glance up fearfully, as if a bomb might be whistling down on them. At times, Salimah felt almost as if each blade of grass in this land had a personal animosity towards her, though looking back later she was appalled at the egotism of this.

She told this to a woman friend from her own country during one of their breaks at work, and the woman gave a loud laugh, then fell silent. Salimah simply sat beside her and said nothing more, but when the work bell sounded her friend glanced round at her, and Salimah saw that she had wiped away a tear. From this moment on, Salimah vowed, whatever the situation she would make it her business to see nothing, hear nothing, remember nothing.

She was clueless about the most basic things. She had no relatives whose help she could call on. She couldn't hope for support from friends. And, worst of all, she couldn't communicate with others. As to what a newcomer like herself could hope for in the way of work, though she could look for it she couldn't really make choices. So, without considering further, she took a job cutting and packaging meat at the local supermarket.

When she first saw the huge slabs of meat, far bigger than herself, that were hanging from the ceiling, she almost cried aloud. The glittering fish skin and the smell of the weirdly shaped shellfish made her gag. But what was harder to bear even than the unpleasantness and stench of the food, harder even than the monotony of the work or the early morning shift, was the scarlet blood smeared everywhere over the stark white tiles of the work place's four walls. It clung there filthy, weary, listless. Whenever she saw it, she averted her eyes as from something horrible. In the desert country where she'd grown up, it was rare to see anything scar or stain the earth. Things left no trace. Perhaps this was why, there, she could somehow bear the sight even of people dying. Now, after a few days' work, she was filled with regret for the way she'd berated her husband, who had begun the same work six months earlier.

Why did you quit?

Okay then, you try it! Actually, you're so stupid you'll probably handle it just fine. Me, I'm not going back there.

A month into the job, Salimah stopped crying. She still came home feeling as if the reek of raw flesh and fish had penetrated deep under her skin, and she stripped off immediately and stood under the shower, but she no longer wept. Again and again she soaked the white work coat in bleach and washed it. But by the time she got home, the blood had caked and hardened into bizarre stains, and she threw herself into contortions scrubbing at the loathsome things with a stiff brush.

With a sidelong disdainful glance, her husband now walked out on her. Having fled here in desperation with his family, he turned around and left his wife and children with barely a shrug. No *Come with me*, no *Wait for me*—he just went. Left on her own to continue the assembly-line grind of living from day to day, Salimah chose nothing more than simply to live, as if she knew no other way than this.

As time went by, things grew less awkward and difficult for her. Life went more smoothly. Her wages rose a little. She was still far from mastering English, but she could now have minimal conversations as needed, and she had both more vocabulary and more skill in handling fish and meat than those around her. When she was first learning, a middle-aged woman, an old hand, had come over from another supermarket and shown her with impressive care how to deal with the slabs of beef and lamb lying on the table before her. Having done this, she handed Salimah a series of knives large and small, each time placing a guiding hand over Salimah's small one and stepping around behind her to encircle her slender body. The smell of her sweat mingled with the reek of flesh, so that Salimah had to choke down the bitter bile that rose in her throat.

Leg, thigh, neck, rump, shank, rib. Liver and frame. Nothing was thrown away. Meat on bones that were too big to handle easily, or cuts that couldn't be sold in the shop front, were allowed to be taken home, Salimah learned. How did people cook these bones and lumps of meat? she asked, and her instructor laughed in genuine amusement. *No no, you give them to the dog*, she replied. *DOG!* she repeated loudly and forcefully, to make sure Salimah understood. *There are lots of farms around here, see, so most people go home to a hungry work dog or two. They're important workers, so they're fed well. What did you do back where you came from?*

Salimah followed her memory back to picture herself working in the field or helping round the house. "Always I was seeing off someone who go to work. With us, not dogs but many children were hungry."

At Salimah's faltering reply, the woman's expression suddenly softened, and she wiped the bloody knife on the corner of the stainless-steel worktop.

"Now you're the one going off to work, aren't you, dear. So who sees you off at the door?"

Nobody saw Salimah off when she set out on foot at 3 A.M. Her sons were taken to school later by a friend who lived in the same public housing block. The arrangement was that Salimah would go to collect both sets of children when she came home each day.

"The moon, mist . . . "

"Okay. Well, at least you're not alone then. That's good."

At her instructor's final words, Salimah suddenly relaxed. She slid her knife in through the red meat. No one had ever spoken to her so kindly before. Now she wanted to make this woman happy in return. She would soon show her how she could cut meat neatly, wasting nothing, just as this woman wanted.

Others who had also left their own country worked alongside her here, and all these women had taken up this battle with the knives after their husbands had, for one reason or another, thrown it in. The men had gone on to get other work of various kinds and learned how to earn their living, but the women were loath to give up work once they'd found it. You could put up with the place when you were used to it. You didn't need more than the absolute minimum of English to get by, and you could chatter away to friends in your own language. The only time they all fell quiet was when the supervisor appeared; everyone shut up as he walked along the aisles, waiting for him to be gone again. Beneath their feet stretched a hygienically tiled floor; the meat dangling from the ceiling and the big boxes of fish gently dripped blood. For the next several months, Salimah concentrated on the task of learning to transform these things with her knife, thoroughly and efficiently, to a point where their original form would be unimaginable.

In the hour when night met morning, Salimah hurried off to work, crunching the hoarfrost as she walked. The car park in front of the work place was already churned and muddy. Others behind her called her name, and they walked together into the concreted space. As she changed in the locker room, Salimah's mind was still on the milky mist and frost outside. That translucency. It cleansed her through and through. Looking around this work place, she registered all its colours as absolute, overpowering, finite. The white of the room, the colour of her own skin, and the colour of blood—these melted away into the pre-dawn air. But here these three colours never mingled. On the contrary, they were as if filmed with oil, remote, resisting approach. Even the white gauze cap she wore felt awkwardly huge and puffed, as if shrinking away from contact with her curly hair, and when she glanced across to the others dressed just like herself, silently working at the meat and fish, and watched how the metallic-smelling blood oozed and blurred at their fingertips, she was seized by the illusion that they were slicing at their own fingers. In fact, they were wearing latex gloves, but these were so thin that they scarcely seemed to exist. Though the gloves were supposed to completely encase their hands, their fingertips still somehow became coated in a fine membrane of blood and sticky fluid. At the sight of it, Salimah felt a shock like a naked hand clutching her heart. She felt suddenly sick, and instantly she sought out her own frail, faint shadow, cast by the fluorescent lights, the only thing that never deserted her. She heard then a sound that only she could hear, a cry that rose from the long row of shadows cast by each of her companions as they worked.

These voiceless screams clung to the windowsills of the work place, seeking a way out. They beat against the windowpanes like little trapped birds, hushed but fierce. Whenever Salimah saw the sunrise outside, the one colour that was no different from her old home, she longed to free these shadows into that fresh bright orange.

Dear teacher,

How are you? I never dreamed that I would receive a telephone call from you. And your first words were "Are you writing?" I wanted to cry! Thank you so much for worrying over me like this. It makes me truly happy.

Time has gone fast, and it's now half a year since we moved here. I'd grown used to living in the city, and I wasn't at all looking forward to moving, but it was a question of my husband's work, so there was really no help for it. The idea of a town by the sea sounds romantic, but in reality, there's a raging wind off the sea (generally mixed with either rain or sleet), and if you leave the car outside, it gets all rusted up, and the only trees around are those thick-leaved eucalypts that grow on this part of the coast, which makes for dull scenery. In the summer tourist season, the population swells to double its size, and things are more cheerful, but for the rest of the year the only colour in the monotonous grey is the gaudy sightseeing boats left abandoned on the shore.

At present, we live in a flat we chose solely for its cheapness. Three flats downstairs and three upstairs, a two-storied building that looks like two bread loaves piled on top of each other. Downstairs lives a truckie (he delivers pet food to Queensland, and comes home once every three weeks), an Indian mother and child (the son is around twenty I'd say), and an old hairdresser who lives on his own (he leaves at exactly eight every morning and comes back at exactly six-thirty, and you can see through the curtains that his room is crammed full of posters of the Virgin Mary, religious medallions and so on). Upstairs is us, then next to us a vacant flat, and beyond it lives a young drummer (unemployed, I'd guess), who's a real problem for us. Our daughter gets woken by the noise of drumming in the mornings and cries terribly. She was born not long after we got here, and she's now over four months old. She keeps me so busy the days pass before I'm aware of it.

My husband is in and out of his university office and teaching all day, and at night he works on his thesis. Before he sits down to it, he spends some time lecturing me on his ideas—he says he needs to gather his thoughts by talking them through in his own language before writing them in English. For the last few weeks I've been immersed in Chomsky with him. He's mad about someone called Gardner, and he tells me he wants to do a study on the possibilities of individual variation in the field of applied linguistics. These nightly lectures have given me a lot more opportunity since I married to think about language. And this innocent country town environment actually suits him down to the ground. He's immersed in his work day and night.

Thank you very much for going through "Francesca" for me. I still get a lot of prepositions wrong, don't I? And my verb tenses are terminal. If anything, they seem to be worse than ever. I hadn't glanced at the manuscript again since I first wrote it back when I was pregnant, but your kind offer to check it for me gave me the impetus to seize every spare moment when my daughter was sleeping to try and write it up into something. I had no idea child-rearing would be so tough! What with all the changes in my life, and becoming a mother, not only my writing but everything

I do tends to feel horribly tangled and rambling now. After my daughter was born, I suddenly began to notice all the superficial things in my writing that I hadn't understood, which means I've lost the strength and frankness of "The Spiders." And though my husband can continue concentrating on his thesis when the baby screams, I can't.

For now, we only have one car, so once my husband sets off in the morning, I have to take a bus if I go anywhere. When we need to go for checkups and vaccination shots, he gives up his lunch hour to drive us to the clinic, but we take the bus home. I've never known a bus to come on time here. I miss those city trams. I wish we had a second car. If only I could get about freely the way I did when I was back there in the city. My husband says we'll be moving back in two or three years, so I just have to put up with it for now. I'm already really looking forward to seeing you again when we do go back.

I'm guessing you're as busy as ever. Are you still teaching academic writing? Joel is taking his VCE this year, isn't he? I hope it all goes well for him.

This is the first time in quite a while that I've felt the urge to write a letter. Stay well.

S.

Twice a week, Salimah began to use the time between coming home, showering, and eating a light lunch, and going off to collect the children, to study at an English language school.

She wore an ankle-length skirt and leather sandals, summer and winter. The simple cotton blouses and T-shirts she picked up at charity shops had nothing to do with current fashions. Sometimes she added a gold necklace. Before she went out, she gave herself a quick spray with eau de cologne. When the scented mist from the nozzle filled the air around her, it seemed to dispel the chilly indifference of her clothes, so that they wrapped her skin more snugly. This was a ritual she'd begun in order to escape from the lingering smell of flesh and fish, but it had an urgency about it that suggested it was a way of connecting her firmly to the everyday world.

No one from her own country went to the language school. All the students in the class were women. There were a number of blondes—not the pale blonde hair that you saw in the local women, but Scandinavians whose silky golden hair framed white faces smooth as new-made porcelain. There was also a healthy-looking olive-skinned woman, apparently Italian, and an Asian with hair as black as Salimah's but hard and straight as an echidna's quills.

This decision to study English on Wednesdays and Fridays was far from being the first time she'd wanted to learn. She remembered the man at the Immigration Office explaining carefully through an interpreter that migrants and refugees were entitled to a number of hours of free English language tuition on arrival. It was just that she couldn't bring herself to ask her husband if she could study. His constant refrain was that women were stupid, so she'd always believed that she was. But she had learned how to handle meat and fish, hadn't she? Still, once the children had begun to pick up the language they could interpret for her, and she had sometimes caught herself thinking she didn't really need to learn English after all.

She had also wondered if she could learn anything new at her age. Her suffering until now had consisted of knowing her own worthlessness, yet she never felt quite reconciled to this idea of herself. She had been utterly terrified, of course, of undergoing new suffering, but there beside the other women, her fingertips dyed with blood like theirs, a single thought had possessed her—that she was different. They had grown accustomed to the work place, to the work, had even successfully adjusted to the everyday round of life that went with it. For Salimah, however, time provided no growing intimacy with the stains on the walls, the grimy sink in the kitchenette. She felt as estranged from it all as ever. She longed to learn how the others did it. Quite likely she would find this same awkwardness in the angular block letters of the English alphabet. She sometimes glanced at her sons' homework and asked a few questions, but they laughed her off scornfully—*You can't even read English, Mum!* The pride she had managed to achieve in herself by learning how to handle meat was trampled underfoot again by this new defeat.

Very well, she said to herself firmly, *I'll do a good job of learning how to handle these harsh English words too.* Yes, she could get by at the work place. But this decision to try going to school to understand the language of this country was so astonishing to her that she could only think it came from that other self she treasured inside her—the dark shadow self that only appeared in sunlight.

There was no beginning, intermediate, or advanced; the motley collection of students gathered in the one room spent their time doing neutral activities that all levels could handle. Faced with Salimah, who could only be called an absolute beginner, the teacher set her at the beginning of each class to read aloud the weather report in the local newspaper. Her pronunciation was riddled with mistakes and close to incomprehensible, but the full, commanding voice that issued from her throat dominated the classroom.

The spring weather largely consisted of strong winds, cloud, and light rain, so in each class she read out much the same words: *Westall-y winds. Strong-wind-war-ning. Mos-tly cloud-y. Show-ers in the arf-ternoon. A mini-mum temp-prature of four de-grees and a maxi-mum of twelve.* The Scandinavians widened their glass-blue eyes and snatched quick conversations together; Olive hung her head and stared in boredom at a spot on the desk. Echidna had opened the paper to the weather report, but her eyes quickly shifted to the brightly coloured advertisements nearby. Salimah trod her way rhythmically through the string of words, hesitantly announcing them one at a time. These first five minutes of the hour-long class were the only time when her sturdy voice was to be heard. When she had finished, the red-haired teacher would read the same place aloud herself as a model.

All right now, everyone?

Westerly winds, strong wind warning, mostly cloudy, showers in the afternoon, a minimum temperature of four degrees and a maximum of twelve, came the chorus. The maidens' voices danced as sweetly as honeyed flowers. Despite her heavy accent, Olive's tone oozed a dignity that came from long years of handling the language. As for meek little Echidna, she murmured the words in a tone as flat as her own face. Salimah went back over what she had read, correcting it mournfully, as if carefully gathering up one by one the broken flower stems of a bouquet that rough children had trampled. *Westall-y winds. Strong-wind-war-ning. Mos-tly cloud-y. Show-ers in the arf-ternoon. A mini-mum temp-prature of four de-grees and a maxi-mum of twelve.*

Though this didn't improve her English much, she loved going to the school. When she walked into the classroom, her shadow suddenly sprang to life and walked along beside her like a friend. It was as if together they were setting out to explore new territory. She hadn't breathed a word of all this to the women at work. It was a secret pleasure, like stoking a basement stove with firewood and returning to the warm upstairs room. Simply reading the weather report aloud at the beginning of class made Salimah feel that she was speaking excellent English.

During work breaks, Salimah would sit there listening to the others chattering on about some delicious food you could get at a certain supermarket and how awful the food was somewhere else, while she stole glances at the patch of sky out the window. Watching the sun slowly rising into the ultramarine sky, its orange tinge spreading, the trapped, despairing feeling that had been haunting her suddenly lifted. She wanted to spring out through the window into the sunlight. It was not so much an urge to escape that scream which could only express itself through the sight and smell of blood and knife. Rather, everything in this work place she had grown so accustomed to had paralysed colours that now suddenly flashed through her like lightning, imbuing her with their hues. She turned her eyes back to the sunrise again. The orange seemed almost to drip fresh and sweet from deep within the slightly oval disc of the sun, to comfort her. Salimah sat there like a cat crouched on the road, listening to her companions chatter on. It was still the same old talk of what you could get where. *Just go along to Y and see, you can get X there*, one was saying happily. *Oh, you can get X at Y,* repeated the others.

You can get X at Y—such simple things made these women happy. But for Salimah, X was a distant dream, while Y felt ungraspable as mist. What she wanted for her own X was to find and hold that orange colour. But where X was she could not even begin to imagine.

"You could call those girls 'nymphs,' I think," murmured Echidna to Salimah and Olive. Salimah liked the word—it seemed to her precisely to express the pristine air of the Scandinavians, the way they looked as if there might be a pair of wings unobtrusively tucked away at their backs.

Echidna didn't talk much, but Salimah had the

impression that she was always a step ahead of her. *She's had good schooling*, Olive said of her protectively (Echidna was the same age as her own daughter). Olive was the epitome of an expansive Italian Mama, and she seemed to feel an urge to enfold tiny Echidna and shield her with her capacious body. As she watched Echidna turn up to class carrying her tiny child, who could still barely control its head, Olive was in the habit of remarking *Poor kid, she came out here knowing no one and now she's had a baby.* Whenever the baby started crying, Echidna would quietly leave the room, then when the cries finally ceased, there she suddenly was again, back in her seat. This happened frequently, but no one in the class complained. Everyone sat up straighter when they saw Echidna. Olive fussed over her, and pushed the fretful baby to and fro in its carriage to soothe it.

"I just want to study," Echidna had announced at the beginning of the term. Salimah envied her, and was pricked with a real jealousy too. Echidna had a husband, and so had an assured household income. True, Salimah too could have gotten a subsidy from the government if she had chosen to apply. She already received a substantial sole parent tax deduction and welfare benefit, but now that she was going to school she might also be eligible for a student benefit. But she didn't feel she should apply for it. It was over a year now since her husband had left, and he hadn't communicated since. But what would people think of her if she said that she was lucky he'd gone, that she was happier now? Her husband would never have understood it if she had said she wanted to study. It seemed to Salimah that Echidna had none of those hard decisions and private difficulties.

"I'm just scared of being left here not knowing the language, no one to look after me or take me places. If I just sit around doing nothing, I'll be an old lady before I know it."

Salimah was dazzled by Echidna's earnest frankness. Olive had told Echidna there was no need to fret like this, but Echidna stubbornly held to her opinion. *You've got an Australian husband, see. The man you spend your days with was your entry into this country. But I have to make my own.*

Salimah listened and wondered. Echidna had come to Australia with her Japanese husband, who was doing postgraduate research at the university, and she had to stay put at home with her baby, without any help or government subsidies. Perhaps English classes were her entry into the country.

In that case, she thought, her own entry had been the work. She thought of the way her hands worked, swiftly and efficiently removing bone, sinew, skin, organs, and transforming a lump of meat into supermarket cuts in a matter of minutes with a single knife. She had never during this past year felt or indeed needed such tenacity of purpose.

Even if the way in was firmly locked, she would twist the door open with that knife. Perhaps then she would find the path to her own X. So she told herself, as she watched Echidna sitting in front of her in class, her back huddled tensely over the notes she was writing, the baby on her lap.

The nymphs had come to Australia as tourists, and they were due to go home again come summer. Those northern European countries looked after their citizens well, and they had an affluent air about them. Their happy future seemed to become tiny particles that imbued their golden hair; it was as if transparent light poured from their bodies, thought Salimah as she looked at them. The delicate wings of light at their backs seemed to unfold, and they were fairies flitting from flower to flower. Just to see them made Salimah's heart swell gently. And then, too, their English was so good. They didn't have the nasal drawl of Australian English; they spoke in the bouncing, clipped British manner, pronouncing the words precisely to the final syllable. It made Salimah feel cheerful just to hear the bell-like voices of these young girls. When she was with them, she felt she had entered a fairy-tale land. She looked on jealously while they airily proclaimed that they'd be going back to university to finish their studies once they went home again.

To go home again. Where could this idea come from? How would it feel? And what kind of place was it that they came from? It's true, thought Salimah, everyone else here could go home if they wanted to. But Olive had been here for almost thirty years, and Echidna said she'd been here for seven. Neither of them had ever spoken about their own countries. They seemed never to have had anywhere to go back to. They could speak quite enough English to get by in everyday life, and Salimah couldn't understand why they were coming to the school to study. But she could see that both of them had turned their backs on the simple formula of "if you go to X you can get Y," and were searching for something more than mere money and time could get them.

Olive was older than the others. Her children had grown up and left, and she said she wanted to relearn

English from the basics up. She could speak it easily, but she still relied on her Australian husband for writing and reading, and she claimed to be hesitant about signing important documents and so on. When Salimah heard her rattling off her skilful English, she listened in silence, too shy to try saying anything herself. Echidna, on the other hand, seldom spoke, but she was good at reading and writing. She explained briefly that she wasn't much good at talking in her own language either. Hearing her faltering voice gave Salimah a quite groundless confidence that she could talk to her.

Olive's husband was close to retirement, she said. She seemed to have put well behind her any urge to get Y at X, not to mention any real fighting spirit—like a veteran player facing her final match, who can afford to sit back on the stands and simply watch from now on.

Echidna, on the other hand, sitting there apologetically in the corner of the classroom with her baby during the hourly lessons twice a week, seemed like someone who was preparing to go out to win or lose—she had a passionate flame in her for *something*, that was sparked by a combination of naivety and a very human aggressiveness. Her husband was doing research, and times were hard for them. Life with a little child was difficult.

She told Salimah she'd love to be working. *You work at a supermarket, don't you? What's it like to work there?* Salimah gazed at her round-eyed with astonishment—at this mother with an infant child, her clean, well-clipped fingertips. Her black hair, thick and straight as stalks of spaghetti, was combed neatly back and held in place with a black hair tie. Her cotton blouse was faded with washing and damp from where her dribbling baby had nuzzled into it. On the desk before her lay her notebook, crammed with English.

All Salimah could think was that this was quite the wrong order. First came work, surely, and then study. That is how to achieve the formula *you can get Y at X*, after all. You made money at work, then learned the language at school. It seemed to her that if you rushed straight off to school, there would never be any hope of a chance to fit in work. Gazing at Echidna with the blazing stare of someone first clapping eyes on a person of a different race, she pronounced in weather-report tones, *You could not do it.*

Then, seeing Echidna turn as if to escape Salimah's gaze and lower her eyes, her hand now playing with the edge of the open white page of her notebook, Salimah murmured, *School suits you better.* She was surprised at how naturally she spoke this time.

D ear teacher,
Thank you for prodding me like that in your last letter. However, I'm sorry to say that I've done absolutely nothing more to "Francesca" since you read it last. My daughter's weaning has been difficult, and I waste my days dithering about trying to come up with suitable food to give her. Tonight, while I was here alone cooking up some rice that I wasn't sure she'd eat, I found myself crying miserably for no reason. I can't write at the moment.

You kindly say that I mustn't stagnate, so if I can't do any creative writing I should write letters to you instead. In fact, writing to you is my only form of encouragement and salvation right now. Apart from anything else, these old-fashioned letters where you stick on a stamp and it gets delivered by hand create a wonderful sense of anticipation, don't they? I find I keep going to check the postbox again and again each day.

My husband is in London for two weeks at the moment. He was worried about leaving me and my daughter here alone when he left, but in fact he's been mentally elsewhere for weeks. His head has been full of preparing for the trip, making teaching materials and handouts and so on. He's had a long teaching stint, and he's been really looking forward to holding workshops with students and colleagues over there. The lectures are given on a voluntary basis, but still, if they invite you,

you do it, even if you have to half kill yourself getting to the other side of the world. It seems to me that there are three Ps that someone must have to accomplish any-thing—Patience, Perseverance, and Passion. And how lucky you are if you can do work that you really love!

I had a fight with that drummer a few days ago. He's at his drums from ten in the morning through until evening, so my daughter can't sleep, and she spends the day grizzling and exhausted from crying. I've asked if he could just hold off making all this noise for a few months, but it doesn't stop no matter how often I beg him. I'm exhausted too, and on this day, I just couldn't take any more of the constant drums and cymbals, and I went and shouted at him. *This is our country,* he shouted back, *why are people like you here? Go back to your own country!* Then I really lost it, and I yelled back abuse at him, though I was so fired up that I've forgotten what I said. It so happened that the truckie downstairs was at home at the time, and when he heard the commotion, he came up and intervened for me. He's a big, powerful man, tattooed all over the upper half of his body. *Hey you!* he yelled at the drummer. *Whaddaya think yer doin' makin' that racket all day? There's a baby here, ya know!* The drummer slammed the door in his face, but there wasn't another sound out of him for the rest of the day.

When I thanked the truckie as he was heading back down the iron staircase, he grinned and said, *I'll shut him up for ya any time I'm around, love.* Next morning the drumming began again, and I heard the truckie come up before I could go out to complain. He banged on the door, and immediately everything went quiet. Then the truckie came round and knocked on my door. *Hey, come on out a sec, will ya?* he said, trying to look small. *There's somethin' I wanna ask.* I went out with my daughter in my arms, and he was sitting there on the staircase with a newspaper spread open on his knees. *I'll keep him quiet as long as I'm about*, he said. *Now could you read this for me?* So I sat down beside him and read out the Sports and Finance columns and the gossip about celebrities, while my daughter slept peacefully in his big arms. *You can hear that I'm not much good at English,* I said to him, but he said I was much easier to understand than the Indian downstairs, so he'd be back for more. He has a son with his estranged wife, but he said these days she's so ashamed of her husband, she avoids seeing him or bringing the boy round.

I've never known anyone who couldn't read before, you know. But I felt as bad for him as if it was me. If you can't even read and write your own language, the inconvenience would be the least of it—you lose your human dignity.

You know, my husband and I came to this country full of hopes and dreams, but the reality has been really hard, and now after seven years, here we still are with barely a penny to our name. And we can only make our way through English. We can only rely on this language in order to be treated as human beings. That's the lesson that this big man's timid little eyes have taught me.

I wonder if I can find an ESL class somewhere in this completely Anglo-Celtic country town. If I can find one, I want to join it. I can't help clinging to the grain of hope that I might have the luck to meet another teacher like you there. While one lives in a foreign country, language's main function is as a means of self-protection and a weapon in one's fight with the world. You can't fight without a weapon. But perhaps it's human instinct that makes it even more imperative to somehow express oneself, convey meaning, connect with others.

I'll rewrite "Francesca" and send it to you, and I'd be

grateful if you would read it. You've told me I must write, and I promise I will. You're the one person who persists in encouraging me.

S.

PS: I think Joel must be about to start his VCE exams. Is his first subject English? The texts when I did it were Frank McCourt's *Angela's Ashes* and E. Annie Proulx's *The Shipping News.* As usual, the Shakespeare play was *Hamlet.* Those exams made me battle the English language more passionately than I'd ever done before. It really taught me how lax I was in the way I relied unthinkingly on my own language. Ever since then, the way I read and write my mother tongue has felt really crude. I'd always just arrogantly assumed I knew it, without ever trying to really come to grips with it. It was dishonest. How much I've realised by learning a foreign language! You learn how to speak and hear, in other words you learn the sounds of a language, through the realities of everyday social life, and it's seared into your ears and tongue forever, most especially through being associated with strong emotions like mental and physical joy or pain.

But the cultivation of the written word, the language that sustains thought, is an individual matter, a thing that endlessly changes as it's propagated inside each person's head. It's like planting the seeds of language deep inside the heart. It's simple when you're young, but with the passing years it can get difficult to dig into the hardened earth. I'm neither young nor very old yet, and my hope is that I can use not only the visual input of reading but the output of writing, however clumsy, till one day a whole forest of language has grown in the soil of my heart.

One day as spring was approaching, Salimah was called in by the supervisor.

Her pay slip had been lying curled in her notice box at work, and when she spread open the yellow sheet of paper she found hidden in it a tiny scrawled note, rolled tight like the fortune in one of those shell-shaped fortune cookies that you get with the bill after a Chinese meal. "Come to the supervisor's room in the break," it said. Salimah's eyes went to the glass-walled office at the far end of the work floor. High up under the great ceiling, a section had been partitioned off into a series of glassed rooms like a row of ice cubes, from which the bosses could instantly check on the workers below. Still, sound couldn't penetrate—the women could enjoy a certain amount of chat as they worked, indeed the bosses were happy to allow a degree of talk, believing that it helped with the monotony of the labour. But they were never allowed to pause. Without appearing to, the supervisors kept a firm eye on the women until they had nimbly cut up all the meat and filled the plastic trays and pallets.

Salimah's immediate supervisor was excellent at his job, sometimes emerging from behind his long glass door to do the rounds of his part of the floor. He changed his shoes for soft-soled gumboots to walk on the tiled floor, so his footsteps were quite inaudible, but as soon as they saw him, the women clamped their mouths shut and concentrated on their hands. The only noise was the steam escaping from the vents, but no sooner had they heard the sound of the glass door closing again than the women burst back into conversation as if returned to life.

It wasn't that they hated him, but they did find his presence uncomfortable. His expressionless eyes could seek out their object with unnerving precision, and his movements were deft and discreet. In the pre-work meetings, he only said what was necessary, no more and no less, without faltering or pausing. The air around his spotless white uniform seemed to repel everything with its brilliance. The women decided he must be single, and had a lot of fun making up stories about a wife who'd left him. The tales took on an almost independent reality among them, but in fact no one knew a thing about his private life. There were times when this ignorance provoked a fear which tipped over into paranoid fantasies. He walked soundlessly behind you in his gumboots. You did your best to avoid him, and if you were in danger of laying eyes on him you would do all you could to exclude him from your vision. He seemed spookily inhuman to Salimah, like some god of death, and this was the name she privately gave him. What did the Death God want with her? she wondered now.

During the morning break she slipped away from the others as if going off to the toilet, and headed for the supervisor's office. She had never spoken to him apart from the initial interview.

He was ready to receive her, standing behind a desk piled with a vast mountain of documents.

Hi, I've been waiting for you. Here you are, take a seat, he said, his welcoming tone very different from the businesslike style of her first interview. Salimah seated herself on the leather sofa in front of the desk. *Right,* he said. He went out, and returned a few minutes later clutching a paper coffee cup in both hands. She had to giggle at his expression of earnest care as he stepped carefully along endeavouring not to spill it. *Here you are,* he said, setting the cup on the glass-topped coffee table. The espresso was topped with creamy white foam. As she took her first sip, he made a short announcement: *You've been chosen as Employee of the Year.*

Salimah gazed at him stupefied.

Evidently taking this to mean she hadn't understood the English, he explained it to her slowly. "You have been chosen as the person who has worked best this year. Your wages will rise a bit, and you will get an additional cash prize."

Salimah listened in bewilderment. *Why had she been chosen?* she asked him. His face froze, and to Salimah's amazement he actually blushed. *You're the first person to ask that,* he intoned softly. He took a sip of his coffee. *Well,* he went on bashfully, *you can tell just from watching you.*

Salimah had no idea how to respond to this, so she too sipped her coffee. He produced a piece of paper for her to sign, and as he gave it to her, his eyes bored into hers. His deep gaze gave her the sensation of a fish caught in a net, and she had to carefully calm her beating heart before she could pick up the pen to write her name. Nobody had ever looked at her like that before, said a silent, hoarse little voice in her dry throat.

Naturally, she had no idea what was written on the piece of paper lying in front of her. Nevertheless, she took her time to read it over, word by word. The ones she knew and the ones she didn't. He simply sat there in front of her, concentrating on her moving eyes. His gaze was not the one with which he watched the women working through the glass—it held an unmistakable intensity and kindness. His hands were held on his lap, the fingers firmly interlaced. The white fingers looked like they were moulded from cold clay models of fingers. Tiny blood vessels were visible in the irises of his blue eyes, red with what seemed a natural admixture of iron. Those two very different colours, the red and the blue, seemed somehow to beg for Salimah's understanding. A man used to killing things—no, trying unsuccessfully to become habituated to killing. An awkward man, who had learned to kill only his own feelings. Look, a man timid as a child. A strange man.

Suddenly Salimah was flooded with a sense of warmth and closeness that she'd never felt for the Death God before. Her mouth widened in a bright ripple of beautiful smile, which spilt over onto the supervisor's face so that he returned it with a soft smile of his own. There was no need for words.

Through the local paper of this small town one learned of indispensable everyday social matters such as which family had had a baby, whose son had just turned twenty-one, who was marrying who where and when. Armed with this information, the readers would send their formal clothes to the cleaners, or buy a birthday card, telephone the bereaved, and gossip on the street corner. The morning following Salimah's meeting with the supervisor was no exception—it ran photos of the local businesses' Employees of the Year. A little photo of Salimah, expressionless, at the time of her first interview, was among the six. Small though it was, it stood out. It was unusual for a photograph of anyone who wasn't a local to appear in the newspaper.

Her workmates pitied Salimah for being a deserted working mother of two, so the looks she met there were full of sympathy rather than envy. Their sympathy disgusted her, but she showed no flicker of this as she thanked them. That afternoon when she went to the language school, Olive came rushing over to her. *Isn't this fabulous!* she exclaimed, her eyes wide with delight. The teacher evidently knew too, and called across her congratulations from where she stood near the whiteboard.

Salimah felt rather jubilant. The poor student who was always set to read the weather report felt she was having her day today.

Echidna hadn't arrived yet. For some reason, Salimah hadn't been looking forward to seeing her after the news, so she was quite relieved when she saw the empty seat. But hearing her name, the teacher looked up, and what she said pierced Salimah to the quick. *I thought she'd be better off studying at the university than coming here. She was a university graduate back home, after all, and she'll be fine here as long as she can write a thesis. And she studies so well. So I told her she should aim higher. They have an excellent childcare centre at the university, too. She'll have gone there today, with my letter of recommendation. I hope it all goes well.*

That day, Salimah couldn't keep her thoughts on the

lesson. She kept thinking of Echidna. She no longer cared about being Employee of the Year. Instead, she was consumed with envious thoughts of that childcare centre, and of the university.

Not long after this Salimah discovered that, for reasons of his own, her supervisor was also coming to the vocational training college where she went for her English classes.

Sitting in the classroom early one afternoon, looking idly out the window beside her before the class began, she saw him crossing the courtyard beyond. An early summer breeze rustled the long leaves of the eucalyptus trees, and the air was rich with the scent of the flowering jasmine that scrambled everywhere over the fence. *Supervisor!* she called boldly. He stopped and looked around, then focused on her and walked slowly over. She had never seen him wearing anything but the standard white work coat and rubber boots, and in jeans and flannel shirt he looked like a different person.

Is this your English class? he asked when he had come into the classroom and sat beside her, seeming quite unsurprised. *Yes*, she replied simply.

Both were rather tongue-tied, and no real conversation passed between them, but it felt as if the fact that they were both at the college was now a secret they shared. There were no further questions on either side; it was enough that they were both outside the work place and looking at things other than cuts of meat and fish. For Salimah it was more than enough simply that the lawn lay before her, yellowy green, edged with colourful flowers in the surrounding garden beds.

Have you gotten used to life here? he asked. But when

she replied that yes, she had finally grown used to both the life and the work, an odd expression crossed his face. *No*, he said, shaking his head. *You're different.*

Why should he think she hadn't got used to the work after all this time? Salimah couldn't imagine what could be different about her, but looking at him there with his brown curls tossed lightly by the breeze, she imagined that he must feel that he himself was somehow different, too.

You're different. And that's good. With these few words, spoken in a way that suggested this time alone together was precious for him, he stood up, resolutely turned, and walked out through the glass doors into the entryway of the neighbouring building.

Salimah sat with chin propped on hand during the class, softly repeating to herself the word *different, different*, pronouncing it as carefully as she could, and strangely irritated by the feeling that whatever she said threatened to become indeed a different thing on her tongue. She looked up to find the teacher looming over her. *I'm going to start giving you some simple homework as of today*, the teacher was saying.

The homework that Salimah carried home that day consisted of simple tasks like copying out the alphabet, unscrambling simple vocabulary, filling in the blanks in short sentences, and writing a short description of some printed pictures. Her sons laughed at her when they saw it, in the same tone as her husband when he declared, *Women are stupid.* The very fact of having homework to do was a major development for Salimah. Despite the boys' mockery, she worked away at it until late in the evening, writing lines of capitals and small letters, unscrambling vocabulary, filling in the blanks, and writing descriptive sentences consisting only of subject and verb. Struggling with these unaccustomed tasks in the quiet of the evening, she nevertheless savoured the transition from fear of the unknown to the joy of knowing. Meanwhile, her mind was haunted by something, she couldn't say just what, that the supervisor had identified that day with the words *You're different*. Her only comfort was the thought that, whatever shape this thing may have, its colour was undoubtedly orange.

Her English teacher gave her fresh homework in the next class, and in the following one, and this continued each week. It seemed much simpler than the homework given to the nymphs and to Olive, but the teacher apparently felt it her mission to set work of an appropriate level for her and mark it meticulously. She had intentionally set Salimah to read the weather reports aloud for a while with the express plan of giving her at least a little confidence in her pronunciation. The first problem to be solved, she'd apparently decided, was that despite Salimah's impressively rich alto voice, uncertainty caused the ends of her words to fade. Of course there was always a chance that Salimah might not be able to withstand this rough and heavy-handed treatment, but the teacher felt a strong desire to help, indeed to save, this dogged student, the very epitome of illiteracy, who came unfailingly to every class.

Thanks perhaps to this dedication, Salimah had reached the point where she could successfully read aloud any weather, and (though she herself hadn't really noticed) her heavy accent was slowly improving under the barrage of repeated correction. It may only have been in the limited vocabulary of weather reports, but her pronunciation had grown considerably smoother. Yet the teacher had no way of knowing that inside the apparent blank of this student of hers, something had been ripped apart. The written homework now filled this gaping hole. One by one these precious sheets of writing were applied like bandages to the cruel wounds inside her. Slowly but surely, like the poultices of Chinese medicine, they began to heal the lacerations.

It was when she was boiling spaghetti one evening that Salimah first became aware that the homework was working. No sooner had her eye lit on the words "Method of Cooking" on the spaghetti package than she had read and understood them. Heart leaping, groping from word to word, she read on. There were many words she couldn't read, but it was certainly more comprehensible than it would once have been. Was this what the supervisor had meant by *different*? she wondered, her cheeks glowing with happiness. Then she took a deep breath, shook her head as he had done, and carefully said, *No, different.* Without conscious effort, she still reverted to her old terrible pronunciation. Steam was gushing from the big saucepan. *No, different. This isn't orange coloured.* That was the murmur she heard at her ear from the shadow that lay, stained with the evening darkness, across the kitchen floor at her feet.

Dear teacher,

I hope you are well. Please congratulate Joel on passing his VCE with a grade of 90. I know you were worried about the score for his Advanced Maths, but an aggregate of 90 is a really fine grade. Will he take a gap year next year? I wish I had taken a gap year, instead of going straight to university. I really wanted time to think things through.

You tell me I should pay a bit more attention to detail in "Francesca." Detail—you've always stated that everything really comes down to detail. "This is too strong," you'll say, or "Not enough adverbs," or "Change adjectives to adverbs." English has such a rich variety of descriptive adjectives, and the only way I can choose among them is to feel my way by judging how they work in real conversations or manners of speech. I do try to keep in mind that each word must be as indispensable as a tile in a mosaic— a bit like the words you so carefully select when you write to me.

Until recently, I've been going to an ESL class at the vocational training college that the government office recommended. Things are different out here in the country. There's only one class, and only one teacher, and all the students study together regardless of level and goal. The only thing we all have in common is the aim of learning

English. I couldn't find anywhere that would look after my daughter while I was in class, so I had to take her with me, but everyone in the class, including the teacher, is a woman, and nobody minded at all if my baby cried and wailed. Paola—one of the other students, who has three grown-up children—often looked after her for me. Or perhaps better to say that she was absolutely itching to look after her. Besides her there were three young girls from Sweden, and one woman named Nakichi who I think is a refugee from the Sudan or Somalia. She works in a supermarket and is a single mother. She was made to read out the weather report at the beginning of each class, and she was so bad it made me squirm for her. She shows no sign of having had any education. I wonder how you would have taught a learner like her.

Our teacher is Miss McDonald, but she told us to call her by her first name, Roslyn. She's an ESL teacher like you, but her style is completely different. Roslyn is young, and she makes really good use of authentic material in class, but she's quite brutal; she rejected a piece of writing I did on the sole grounds that there was a misplaced colon, and she was always correcting Nakichi's pronunciation in front of everyone. Maybe part of the reason she's like this is the extreme differences in level among the students.

Roslyn said I must be bored in this class, and suggested I move to the ESL class at the university. She also said there's a childcare centre there for the baby. So I followed her advice and went for an interview with the coordinator. When I showed her my VCE and ELTS scores, she advised me to take the coursework for a master's degree, since I already had a degree. It's a small campus, but luckily there's a solid humanities program. This has meant that I can take up the study I'd abandoned with the move here. But the fees are expensive, so I'm going to start by doing just one course at a time. And then there's the baby, of course.

As usual, the young students who are armed with English as their mother tongue run rings round me in discussions, and I can't utter a word. Their eloquence and effusiveness seem able to transform a simple and unarguable fact, such as "there was a single tree," into the illusion that there were a hundred trees. After a while, the tutor said he wanted a word with me. I went to his room in trepidation at the thought that he would criticise me for being so silent in tutorials, but he didn't mention it. Instead he told me I should change from course work to research since I seemed to be better suited to pursuing my own chosen field of study. He added that I should come and have tea with him once a week. I'm the kind of inept person who can only reach the place I ought to be by failing at the first place I try. After all, you were the one who invited me over to the academic writing course from the ESL Business English course, and who then encouraged me in creative writing, weren't you.

So since then, I've been spending the half hour after class before I pick up my daughter at the childcare centre calling in on Dr. O'Brien (he says to call him Neil), the Art History lecturer, for tea and conversation. I forget time while we're talking. The other day, he really threw me by posing the abstract question "What is beauty for you?" When I replied, "Beauty is what's right. It's Justice," he laughed so loudly that the room shook. He's now invited me to have dinner at home with his family next time.

I sometimes see my husband in the school grounds too. He seems to really enjoy the way the students pronounce his name as "Dr. It" instead of Itô, and he beams from ear to ear. Well, when I look back on how hard he's worked to get here, I can see why.

My daughter is now seven months old, and she's used to going to the childcare centre once a week. I was just beginning to relax because she'd finally learned to eat solids, when she caught her first cold. It was exactly as I'd been told—if you put her into a childcare centre she'll keep coming home with illnesses. She is still sniffly. My husband is hovering over her waiting for her to say her first word. Once she starts talking, he's full of great plans to talk to her using the rules of her own unique language, and note down absolutely everything. The things she says will be his most intimate sample.

Speaking of which, the truckie has asked me to read him E.B. White's *Charlotte's Web*. He gets the drummer to shut up, and we sit on the stairs while he holds my sleeping baby. You know the book, it's that famous children's book that features the grey spider called Charlotte. He said he'd noticed his son reading it. I know the book well—you remember I got the idea for my story "The Spiders" from it? The truckie is a big man, but he cries easily. Every time I read him a chapter, he sheds a tear at the thought that his own son can read such a wonderful book like this all by himself. I'd been hesitating to say anything, but I took the opportunity to ask about the amazing tattoos that I'd noticed, and he told me that his friend had done them for him while they were in jail together. *How on earth?* I asked, unable to hide my surprise. He just grinned and said, *I may not be able to do things other people can, but there are things I can do that other people can't*, and he wouldn't say any more.

From time to time I think of my classmates back at the vocational training college where I used to study English. Leaving aside the class itself, I was just beginning to talk to Paola and Nakichi, and I'm a bit sad that I pulled out halfway through. I do sometimes meet Paola even now.

She's a really fine person, but both Nakichi and I were quite tongue-tied in front of her. No matter how badly you wield something, after thirty years you get to be pretty good at handling it, and her English is quite forceful. The power of it rather overwhelms me, and it gives me an idea of just how she's gotten by in Australia these thirty years. I've recently begun to take on her pronunciation and the way she talks, and now I'm used to it so I can understand her well and don't mind its oddness, even if she sounds unnatural to others. My husband says this linguistic phenomenon is called "fossilisation." That's right, fossilisation. Awful, isn't it. These scholars are so proud of their analytical tools, but they have no idea how it can turn someone's heart to stone to be classified like that. You mean to say that Nakichi and I, who have come to grips with English as a second language in adulthood, will always speak a "fossilised" form of it no matter how we struggle?

Paola has invited me to her home several times. Every eave is draped with drying homemade pasta. She has a fabulous garden, and she's very proud of the rose garden that won a blue ribbon a few years ago. The English box hedge cut in the shape of a charming lollipop is an eye-catcher. I think it was Karel Čapek who said that you have to have reached a certain age before you can make a garden. With a garden like that, you have to be brave enough to pit your chances against the unreliable nature of plants and climate. You have to be virtually enlightened to achieve it.

When I go to visit, I usually leave my daughter to nap in Paola's daughter's old room (the sound of drumming is awful back at home, so this is a real help). She gobbles up the broken bits of Paola's homemade pasta (why doesn't she like the rice soup I make for her at home I wonder?), and I sit there listening to her endless flow of talk until her husband comes home in the evening (he seems a really gentle man). Her three children live in Cairns, Sydney, and Hong Kong, and apparently she hardly ever sees them. These days she doesn't feel inclined to do much, she says, and has trouble getting up in the morning. I'm sure she must be lonely. If only that was all there was to it. Writing about her like this, it seems to me now that it's not only Paola's English that has fossilised, but she herself.

I've rambled on today. Is this the sort of thing you mean by saying I should write details? Incidentally, Roslyn has wiry red hair, which trembles like a flame when she laughs her trailing, drawn-out laugh. Every time Roslyn laughs, Nakichi trembles like a terrified little animal caught in a trap. Poor Nakichi. Maybe she thinks she's being laughed at, though that's not the case. I can tell that she's intently searching for something, though she's not aware of it. Even if she doesn't achieve it, I suspect she'll gain something precious in the process, something she can keep. She's definitely one of those rare people who doesn't use her race or nationality or circumstances as an excuse, in fact has nothing to do with excuses at all.

I'll finish now, and write again later.

S.

To: All
From: Hiroyuki and Sayuri Ito
Subject: Personal Notice
26/2/2004 9:25 P.M.

Dearest friends,

Ito, Yume Noel, 12th December, 2002–24th February, 2004

Our precious daughter, Yume, passed away suddenly (SIDS) at Port Griffin on 24th February, 2004.

Private service and cremation.

Sincere thanks for your support and understanding in this difficult time.

C hief to the supervisor's office, please."
The announcement calling Salimah to the office came over the loudspeaker as soon as the break had begun. The short summer had sped by, and the autumn winds had begun to blow. It was almost two years since she had begun work. A number of her old colleagues had vanished, changing jobs or moving elsewhere. Among those who'd stayed, Salimah had a reputation for being particularly fast and precise at her job, and now she had become the one to train newcomers in the art of handling the meat and fish. She had even reached the point where she could judge from experience and intuition whether the newcomer, be it refugee or high school student, was the type who would turn up for work again the following day.

That morning, before dawn had even broken, it was with shock and displeasure that she came face-to-face with the newcomer who the supervisor introduced. People often said that you couldn't tell one Asian from another, but she had no trouble if it was someone she knew. Echidna remembered Salimah well too, and she stood beside the supervisor looking a mixture of surprised, relieved, and embarrassed. *This is Salimah, the chief worker. She'll be instructing you.* The supervisor spoke to

Echidna in a businesslike way, just as he had to Salimah that first day. Over her arm, Echidna carried a freshly cleaned white uniform.

Salimah led her to the locker room. They were both silent. Salimah's shadow loomed oppressively over this little Asian woman. For her part, Salimah was savouring the pleasurable silence. Here she was, someone who could only envy this "well-educated" woman her university and childcare centre, and Salimah now would be teaching her! There was a distinct pleasure in the thought, and a temptation to throw her weight around when she instructed her. But bathed in this enjoyable sense of superiority though she was, she knew with absolute clarity that there was something *different* about this woman being here. *You're different*, she whispered in her mind, watching Echidna turn away from her to open the locker she'd been assigned, and finally she spoke. *Weren't you taking your baby to the childcare centre and going to university?* Later she regretted these poisoned words, but at the time she simply received a shock like a blow to the head when Echidna replied, *My baby died.*

Her speech was as flat as always. The row of words she strung together seemed to hold no trace of sorrow. *She had just turned one. She'd been put to sleep at the childcare centre facedown, and she died.* The young mother was speaking with a measured tone, like someone relentlessly hammering in nail after nail. *I've had enough*, she continued in a monotone. *Of university, of study, maybe even of my family. I wanted to find some good work. I wanted to be able to hold the gaze of anyone who laughed at me. But my child died. The only thing that I can hang onto in this country now is money.*

As she spoke, Echidna was deftly putting on the white coat and gumboots, and she now stood gazing expressionlessly at her instructor, with the air of one who was ready and waiting. Her dull black eyes below their oriental eyelids did not so much as flinch. Gently Salimah reached out and ran her hand through Echidna's straight black hair, gathered neatly into a ponytail behind her. Echidna looked up at her, startled. *You're a fool. A fool. Just because your child has died, this is still no place for you to come.* Salimah's fierce voice echoed out into the corridor.

Yes, I'm a fool, Echidna repeated, choking with tears. *A fool. To abandon my child to die in that cold unloving bed at the childcare centre so that I could study. If only I hadn't gotten those stupid ideas, but had stayed at home with her!* As she spoke her voice rose to a shout that startled Salimah, then the wave of ferocity subsided again to her usual artless string of simple English, spoken earnestly. *My husband is repulsive! Out there in the world, doing just as he pleases, and he goes about boasting of how he's supporting his family! And when I tried to look after this man's child, she just wailed and resented it. Yes, that's right, I had a child! So I wasn't all alone.*

At the words "all alone," Salimah shuddered. She suddenly understood: despite her sons she was all alone, and the next instant, terror flooded her. She sought her own shadow under the dim fluorescent light. It had loomed so large as she walked down the corridor, but now it seemed to melt aimlessly into the bare concrete around her. Suddenly, rage and sorrow threatened to engulf her.

But it's not right that you're here. It's completely wrong. Salimah spoke with low intensity, her quivering lips pressed to Echidna's temples as she hugged her trembling shoulders. Echidna pressed her face against Salimah's breast and closed her tear-filled eyes. *All I want is to work here and sleep without thinking*, she murmured. Her bitter tears fell in torrents, unstoppable as an endless rain.

For the next few months, unwillingly, Salimah did her best to instruct Echidna in the work and its rules. Echidna was fundamentally earnest, diligent, and persevering, so she very quickly learned to perform the work correctly and even earned herself a reward for effort. Yet she remained expressionless, head bent, apparently unhappy.

But as the autumn drew on, the two grew able to talk to each other as equals at work, even to joke together. What Salimah most treasured was that Echidna could check her now quite difficult English homework. Whenever she came up against something she didn't understand, Echidna was there to help. Her reply to any question was usually instantaneous, and if she did need a moment or two to think she would conscientiously read the sentence over several times to get it to make sense. Whenever Salimah observed her intent and earnest face, bent over the page she gazed at, one hand gently holding back the wiry black hair that hung over her forehead, she would murmur, *You shouldn't be here*, but if Echidna noticed, she would just grin, and she made no attempt to leave. *I like it here. I mean, I've got you here, haven't I?* she told Salimah, quite without embarrassment. And in her heart Salimah replied, *You may be right. You have someone keeping an eye on you here.*

The nymphs had gone back to Scandinavia, and Olive had chosen her moment to leave the class when her husband retired from work, so only a few young Eastern European students and Salimah remained. The students were there with the aim of one day passing the entrance exams for a university course, and a specially trained examinations teacher was employed to coach them. For a while, the lessons continued with only Salimah and her teacher.

One day, Salimah took Echidna to see her red-haired English teacher, and they spent the whole afternoon talking with her abut non-classroom matters. Warm air poured out from the oil heater against the wall, and the window above was white with steam. The teacher had learned from Salimah what had happened to Echidna, and when she saw her framed in the doorway of the classroom, her lacquer-black hair draping her face to the shoulders like a hood, the teacher ran to hug her. *Thank you for coming back*, she said huskily. *What about coming here to study again if you want?* She nodded again and again, her throat catching.

And so it was that all that winter the three held a class together.

Late one night, the telephone rang. Salimah was still not very comfortable talking on the telephone, and most phone calls that came around dinnertime were pointless ones to do with sales or charity donations or marketing, so she would generally let it ring out. But this time the call came later, when her homework was done and she was about to snuggle down into bed for the night, and she had a feeling that someone had something they wanted to tell her.

When she picked up the phone she heard a familiar voice say rather formally, *Hullo? Hullo?* Her husband. Why should he be ringing now? It was more than two years since he'd walked out on them, and the lack of any communication since then meant they could now legally divorce anytime they wanted. Normally, no thought of her husband ever crossed her mind these days, but her older son was now on the verge of adolescence and had recently grown noticeably like his father, right down to the scornful tone of voice he used to his mother, so that it felt to Salimah as if she was living with a smaller version of the man she'd married.

The voice she heard through the telephone, however, was different from her son's, more of a middle-aged mumble that provoked a surprising sense of nostalgia in her. She asked where he was and what he was doing these days. He replied shortly that he was going delivery work in the city, and asked how his sons were going. *Surely not!* she thought, and asked disbelievingly if he wanted to meet them. Caught off-guard, her husband paused, searching for words, then blurted out roughly, *That's right. Any problem with that? They're my sons, after all.* Salimah switched the receiver to her other hand, astonished by what she heard. *It's been two and a half years, you know. How old's the older one now? The younger one? Tell me exactly.* Salimah's voice threatened to rise with the ferocity of her anger, but she stifled it, aware of the two boys sleeping in their bunk beds nearby. *Eleven and eight,* their father announced correctly. *You're just the same, aren't you. Asking what age they are—you mean you can't count for yourself, for god's sake?*

Salimah couldn't sleep a wink that night. It was hard to

be deprived of yet more sleep when her mornings were early enough already, but sleep evaded her.

She counted painstakingly in the dark: *One, two.* Back where she came from not many people knew their own precise age. Salimah had been born in a bad famine year, so her mother had used that as a means to keep track of her age. *Nine, ten.* Up to around that age she'd gone to school and helped with the housework, but after that they'd been burned out and forced to flee from one place to the next, and she couldn't clearly remember what she'd done. *Fifteen, sixteen.* Around that time, she'd spent many weeks in wandering, and had seen her first river. The younger of her little brothers was unable to withstand the feverish hell of his thirst. He'd been told that once he crossed the river, there'd be food on the other side, but he was more desperate to drink the water there in front of him, and he plunged into the river and drank until his thirst was sated. The long journey without food or water had weakened him badly, and his body couldn't cope with the river water. It was her husband who had buried her little brother there beside the river. He'd dug a deep, dark hole for him, so that the wild animals that feed on dead flesh in the night wouldn't dig up his corpse. He had seemed to her a good man.

Seventeen. Having counted through the numbers to here, Salimah suddenly sealed her lips. This was the age when she had become his property. The following year her son was born, and in between they had continued to be swept along in the mass migration. Where was it her younger son had been born? All she could remember was that it was on a grubby blanket. All connection between memory and reality was so confusingly tangled that she couldn't even recall what her age had been then. Then she had come here, yes, when she was twenty-five.

Twenty-six, twenty-seven, twenty-eight. Salimah was now counting in English. Her accent was still strong, but she spoke well enough to be understood. At twenty-six she'd landed a job. At twenty-seven she'd begun going to class. At twenty-eight she'd become the chief of her work place. Every year, every season she had been here, she could remember as if it was yesterday the choices she had made and the things she had striven to attain. Salimah chuckled softly with amusement to think of it; her low laughter floated off in the moonlight, wafting through the quiet room where she lay. At twenty-six she'd sworn to force herself to see nothing, hear nothing, remember nothing—yet hadn't she seen what there was to see, heard what there was to hear, and remembered all there was to remember? She had no recollection at all of that time when she'd left her home, resigned to the facts of her life, or the time she had first arrived on these shores. But ever since she had been given the chance to choose for herself, she had asked herself each step of the way only what it was that she herself wanted to do. In this story, her husband did not exist.

Twenty-nine. Salimah couldn't simply let this number drift by. She now knew every inch of her work place, from the factory floor to the cold room below and up to the roof where the male and female workers would sneak off for private embraces away from other eyes. But she had no need to know anything more about her husband. She was simply aware, somewhere below consciousness, of the fact that he was the father of her sons, and that he had never really been interested in his wife. She had been no more than his "mate" in the crudest sense.

Now that he had demanded that she put him in touch with his sons again, she was startled to realise that she still had some connection with him. He had told her she depended on him for everything in life, and she had believed it. Salimah imagined the sons she might be about to lose, running to greet their father. Fresh surprise came with the thought that now slid across her mind—that she had been alone from the beginning, so nothing would really change. She hoped she had brought them up lovingly, she told herself, but when it came down to it children were not possessions. Yet it filled her with sorrow to lose them. Salimah's chest tightened with pain to recall Echidna's bitter laugh as she declared that it had taken losing her child to make her a mother.

Salimah spoke to no one about this telephone conversation, and even kept it from her sons until the very day her husband appeared on the country railway station platform to meet them a few weeks later. At twenty-nine, it was not on her agenda to pore over the details and get sentimental.

From the moment her sons returned from days of breathing the air of the big city where her husband now lived, they were both eager to go back. Their cruel honesty hurt Salimah deeply. But needless to say, it also wasn't on her agenda to go weeping on someone's breast about her pain. Salimah had no intention of letting anyone stand in the way of this business of living that she had finally grasped. She could no longer stand the insult and intimidation that goes under the name of a certain sort of kindness, as when a shop assistant criticises the dress you've tried on and liked and substitutes another in its place. She had no desire to let go of the self she had finally seized hold of. Even if it meant having her sons taken from her.

D ear teacher,
It's been a while since I wrote.
Thank you for your card, phone call, and long letter when my daughter died. I planned to write back straightaway, but for a while I couldn't think let alone write in either Japanese or English.

My husband left for Boston yesterday as planned. It's a one-month study trip that's been arranged since last year, and he was looking forward to it. I wanted to be able to give him at least a bit of extra money for the trip, but what with the funeral (a simple ceremony with just the two of us present) and all manner of other expenses, we have hardly any spare cash.

Sometimes, you know, I open the porcelain lid of my daughter's urn and gaze at her ashes. Most people in this area are buried, but cremation costs less. When the coffin lid was closed, my husband wept aloud. This is a man who didn't cry when his own mother died. Our daughter was born while he was away on business in Dalian. She died quietly, without causing anyone any trouble. She was born alone and died alone. She thought the only way she could be loved was by disappearing from our lives. It was a punishment on us, for being so focused on doing the things we wanted to do.

She had caught a slight cold that day, and I was tossing

up whether to take her to the doctor. We still only have temporary resident visas, so there was no health insurance, and into my mind crept the thought of the money for several weeks' worth of food. I chose not to go to the doctor but to leave her in the childcare centre while I went to class. After class, I stayed to talk with Neil in his room. What is it that you feel makes something a work of art? he asked, and I replied, Colour. I'm moved by colour itself, I said, because it doesn't lie or deceive. Then I went to the childcare centre to get my daughter and found the place in an uproar, because they'd noticed that one of the babies had stopped breathing, but even when they told me it was my child, even when I saw my daughter who would never wake again, I found myself thinking that they were joking or lying, and when the ambulance arrived, it seemed like some elaborate performance.

But my daughter's death was no joke, no lie, and it has smothered my head deep under a whiteness impenetrable as ash. It is the reality of this unbearable sorrow, looming over me like a silently building snowdrift, higher and higher with each passing day, that has finally made me a mother.

Unable to withstand being alone, I sought out Paola at her house so that I could collapse like a child while she stroked my head, but it was her husband who came to the door to tell me that she'd gone back to Italy for a visit. She'd developed what they call depression, he said, and just kept saying she wanted to die, so he had sent her back to her relatives for a healing change of scene. Whenever I saw her, the thought used to flash through my mind that I didn't want to become like her, and now I think I must have been unconsciously foreseeing the way things would turn out for her. I can remember like it was yesterday the Paola who had come to this country to marry and was worrying about what she could do now that her children had flown the nest. The garden that was her pride and joy had grown cruelly bedraggled. Brilliant blue hydrangeas were flowering by the front door. I'd helped her to add a special fertilizer around the roots while she explained that it would make them bloom as blue as the sea. All I managed to say to her husband was a request that she get in touch once she was back.

It was my choice. I chose to let my child die. She was crushed beneath her mother's ego. Her ashes are only a tiny pile at the bottom of the big funeral urn. The man at the funeral parlour said that a big man would overflow the urn. How can I fill this emptiness, this empty urn's worth of a lifetime that should have been hers? No, ash is not cold. A corpse is cold through and through. Hard as metal, chill to the marrow. Yet whenever I let the ash slide through my fingers it grows warm. I can sit doing that so long that I forget time and the passing moments. These days the beat of the drum pins me to this world; the sound of the downstairs hairdresser's car starting as he goes to work in the morning and stopping when he comes home in the evening serves to call me back to the real world of the present moment. I loathe my own humanity and self—my own body as it rises from bed; my face in the mirror; my breathing and eating and evacuating flesh; the self who goes out shopping and counts up the cash; the social self who converses with others as necessary; my emotions, that strive to make me authentically myself by weeping tears in response to my need of a way to be sad, and can do nothing else. All that wrongness, all those worthless things—it's my own human existence itself that I detest.

I haven't been to the university since what happened to my daughter, though Neil did keep telling me I should somehow bring myself to go again. By the beginning of the new semester I'd written the first draft of my thesis. I was given four weeks' special extension, but in the end, I didn't complete the writing.

There was no telling what I'd do cooped up at home the way I was, and besides, we were really strapped for money, so I sent my CV off at random in answer to whatever work I saw advertised in the local newspaper, but there wasn't a single response. On a hunch, I looked in the telephone book, found the most common family name in the town (McKenzie), made up the convincing-sounding name Natalie McKenzie, and applied again, and from the following morning the telephone rang non-stop. I'd never dreamed that my name had acted as a trigger for prejudice. Racial prejudice is based on skin colour, so it's easy to pick, and it can and should be openly confronted. But how do you identify prejudice based on a name?

Anyway, I don't have the strength to pursue this problem right now, so I gave up on the whole idea. Instead, at the supermarket where I do my shopping, my eye fell on an ad on the door that said "Part-time worker wanted to process perishable foodstuffs, no experience required," and almost on impulse, I dashed to the counter and told the shop assistant that I was interested in the job. I couldn't help noticing his unpleasant smile when he registered my accent and the way I talked. So after skin colour and name comes language, I thought in disgust. If men are truly equal, surely language should be equal, too. As I waited while he left his seat to go and fetch the employment officer I was close to tears, wondering whether my daughter was treated equally in heaven, and thinking how I'd let her die before she had even found her first words. For all my impulse to go and protect her, I'm obliged to stay alive here in order to perfect the intricate artwork that is a human life.

Nakichi was at my new work place. She was always so timid in the English class, just set to read the weather report over and over like a naughty child who's made to stand in the corner, but here she's an impressive work place boss. She's taught me all sorts of things, from how to wield a knife and how to cut meat to how to pack and shelve goods. During the break, she brings along her English homework and asks me to help her with the things she doesn't know. I suggested she look things up in the dictionary, but her native language is tribal, and though she says she's learned some Arabic, she couldn't get to the classes properly because of the chaos in her country, so she is effectively illiterate you might say. (in other words, even if there was a dictionary in her native language, she couldn't read it. I imagine Roslyn will coach her in using an English-language dictionary sometime.)

She's in a stronger position than the truckie, because at least she has a second language. Every day another weak little language becomes extinct. English is so powerful today that any language that belongs to a land without economic or political clout must bow at the feet of this vast monster. But any acquired second language will always be dragged down by one's first language. We trust our first language most because it directly expresses our culture and our ways of thought. Actually, without an absolute faith in a first language you cannot nurture a second one. But it seems to me that this second language acquisition (English, in the case of us ESL students) can actually give birth to new values and ways of expressing oneself. Offensive though I may seem to some, I don't deserve that unpleasant smile I received. For someone like Nakichi, whose native land has been taken from her, a second language is a second chance. When I see how zealously Nakichi has committed herself to seizing it, I find myself praying for the possibility of the pure power of language.

I really am all alone now. For a while my husband would rush back as soon as work finished, fearful that I might have hanged myself here while he was gone. But even when he's around, I'm still alone. He has work that he has devoted his life to. His daughter has died, but still, he can immerse himself in work and bring back the wages to support his family. He has those "three Ps" that I wrote of, while I have nothing. I did my best to farewell him as usual when he went to Boston, but my heart was full of bitterness. If it weren't for him I wouldn't have come here. I know I can only go on by being at his side, but I hate it.

S.

I'm hoping you might agree to talk to the class a little about your country."

Salimah's younger son's teacher had approached her when she went to pick the boys up from school. The children had come hurtling out of the classroom with the sound of the final bell, and now the young woman stood straight-backed before her.

It had been arranged that the boys would evacuate to the city to be with their father ("evacuate" was the word used by her friends for moving to the city). A de facto divorce had been recognised and Salimah would soon be on her own, far from everyone she had called family. Some of her friends at work looked puzzled and wondered why she wasn't moving to the city with the boys; others shook their heads knowingly and said she could never have made up for that two-year gap in relations, while others who knew her salary smiled snidely, implying that it was only natural she would want to stay for the money. No matter what they said, no matter what she heard, Salimah remained resolute. No, that's not quite true, for she did waver when a woman rebuked her with the comment that she was unmotherly. But once Echidna had set her right with the crisp observation that this woman was hardly a paragon of motherhood herself, the remark became for Salimah just a passing slur.

It was at this point that Salimah found herself confronted by the youthful, politely spoken teacher. She tensed.

Would you be willing to talk about this before your boys change schools? We're studying the topic of "our multicultural society" at the moment, you see, and I'm hoping that you could provide a perspective on Africa that we wouldn't get from the available materials. The children could do their project work based on your story. We'd love to send it on to your son once it's done.

She could find no reason to refuse. She herself was living a kind of dream existence in which she seemed no longer to have a native land, and she had never said much to the boys, particularly the younger one, about where they'd come from. She had a firm belief that no matter how she tried to express it, she couldn't present their home to them. But now, as she gazed into this young woman's grey eyes, the thought struck her that somehow the time had now arrived when she must do it, and particularly for her younger son, still so little, before she let him go.

He would soon become a young man, after all. He wouldn't forget. Surely it was okay to tell him now, that he had been born on a dirty blanket in the midst of turmoil.

There were a bare two weeks before she was set to appear as a "guest speaker." Salimah tentatively confessed the news to her English teacher and Echidna in the next class. She was worried how comprehensible her English would be to the children, she admitted. Her teacher suggested some project work for homework to help her prepare for her school appearance. She should practice by writing a script entitled "My Home" for a small presentation with the aid of photographs and other audio-visual material that would appeal to people.

Standing under the steaming shower after work, Salimah pondered how to write a presentation that would flow, mentally moving it forward by arranging like chess pieces the things she knew and wanted to convey. But it was too difficult. She went to Echidna for help, and her friend led Salimah to a computer in a corner of the audio-visual room at the town's library and began to search for material on her home country. *Is this what your country's like?* she exclaimed with an astonished sigh, peering at the glowing blue screen. Salimah beside her began to gaze at the screen, as if drinking it in, while Echidna fed coin after coin into the printer slot to print out everything she came across. When Salimah tried to pay, Echidna just smiled silently and shook her head. Then she sorted the pages into sections, snapped each briskly together with a stapler, and used a highlighter to mark the places that Salimah wanted.

Salimah was touched by Echidna's scrupulous efficiency and above all by her thoughtful kindness. She stood gazing for a while almost with emotion at the tips of those thin fingers, appearing and disappearing as they flipped through the white pages, ten dexterous fingers swift as hummingbirds. Echidna clearly loved this activity and never grew bored with it, and Salimah found herself wishing she could convince her to go back to university. Poor Echidna, blaming herself for her child's death, had lost all confidence and had lost herself as well in fact. Here was a precious friend who was unstintingly devoting time and effort on her behalf, and Salimah now longed to do something for her in turn.

After dinner, while the boys spread their homework out on the kitchen table, Salimah sat beside them struggling with this material. Sadly, though, what she found written there was merely cold information, not the life she herself had known. After the boys were sleeping soundly and she had read everything through, that home felt even more like a hazy dream. The following evening, she wrote a short piece herself. This became a cramped text crowded with her teacher's corrections, but she copied it out with a pen a number of times on fresh paper according to her teacher's instructions. Echidna typed it up for her. What had been handwritten words now became a printed text, with a new air of tight cohesion to it. Still she felt something was lacking. Finally, with her son's crayons she drew in the space at the bottom of the page a picture of the sun that had risen and sunk over the horizon through all her days since childhood.

The first thing she did the following morning in the locker room was show it to Echidna. Echidna turned the pages silently before announcing with a smile that she'd done a magnificent job. Then she returned to the final drawing of sun and sand, and stared at it for a while. *This is the same sun that shone on my own country, too, morning and evening. The very same one. But I believed it was a special one that only I saw.*

The day before D-day, Salimah and Echidna put their heads together with their English teacher's red head to polish Salimah's essay. The teacher had planned to get her to present it with writing in hand, but this proved unnecessary. It was no more than an artless string of childlike words, but for that very reason it carried a fresh impact every time the page was turned. Over the course of her career, she had taught English to students from all manner of nationality and linguistic background, but though many sighed for their homeland and idealized it in their minds, Salimah was not one of them. The theme might have been "my native land," but Salimah had no consciousness of concepts such as homeland or country. All she wrote about was what had happened to her. "I sent my little brothers outside to play and I played with them." "We raced and sang songs." Not a single additional word described how it felt—no pleasure, sorrow, loneliness, or delight was mentioned. What had this little girl thought? She had helped her parents and played with her siblings, she had gone off to school. The teacher suddenly felt the grimy layers of tired assumptions accumulated over long years of familiarity lift from her mind: for all the differences of culture and religion, people's lives were much the same everywhere. The conclusion of the piece was also abrupt and stark, but despite the rough, jolting prose, words slapped down like heavy slabs of meat, it had a powerful ring to it. The title "My Native Land" somehow didn't seem to fit.

The teacher drew a double line through the title with a thick felt-tipped pen. Salimah flinched as she watched the pen tip, wondering what the teacher had taken exception to, and turned her eyes to the teacher's face. After blinking thoughtfully a few times, the teacher instead wrote the word "Salimah," and the piece was finished.

Out in the college courtyard garden taking a quick break, Salimah noticed the figure of her work supervisor strolling from right to left through the bushes. Being with her teacher and Echidna, she hesitated to call out to him, but at that moment her teacher suddenly hailed him loudly. He gazed about him, his lower half hidden by the bushes. This was just like the last time, Salimah thought, cheeks flushing warmly. His apprehensive look suggested a petty thief discovered in someone's house. The chill image that he presented in the work place melted now in the warm afternoon sun. When his eyes lit on the three of them, he bashfully walked over. Even Echidna was looking at him like a stranger. Without the white coat and gumboots she barely recognised him, and it was natural that her eyes should widen at this vision of him in grey parka, blue jeans, and sneakers.

"How's it going? Well?"

At the teacher's searching question, he flinched like a boy. In the pale late winter sunlight, his shadow stretched the length of his body over the lawn. Salimah's eyes fell on her own shadow. *Go on, go and talk to him*, she told it silently. The teacher's eyes leapt to her students.

"This is my cousin."

"So these are your students, are they?"

Now the teacher's eyes moved inquiringly among all three in turn. *Do you know each other?* Echidna laughed as she explained, *He's our work supervisor.* She wasn't laughing at the fact that they knew each other, Salimah guessed, but at how different he now looked.

"Actually, you know . . . " the teacher began, but the supervisor put his hand quickly over her mouth before she could say more.

"Oh, there's a secret." Echidna was being uncharacteristically bold. A secret, yes. Just what was the supervisor doing here?

"Letting a few people in on it will just put you on your

mettle and stop you failing, you know," said the teacher as she pushed her cousin's hand away. "He's here to get a driving license," she went on. "You know that mechanic's course, the one with the big garage? He's doing his training there."

The car mechanic's training department was located at one corner of the courtyard. A number of impressively flashy cars were always parked there, constantly surrounded by a gaggle of teenage boys in mechanics' clothes.

At his cousin's words the supervisor turned bright red and stood there stock-still and mute. It wasn't normal for someone of his age not to have ever thought about learning to drive, she went on, but he dismissed this accusation with the simple statement that it hadn't been necessary until now. Salimah was sorry that he'd returned to his usual curt work place mode, and felt an urge to drop in some comment that would soften him, but he had turned and left before she could open her mouth.

The teacher went on to talk about him, referring to him with a sigh as "that kid." Salimah was a little shocked. She felt oddly uncomfortable with the intimate and dismissive way they spoke of each other. "He left high school at sixteen and started work, so he was fending for himself from an early age," she explained. "But he's a weirdo and people find him a bit unapproachable."

Salimah didn't understand this word *weirdo*. She glanced sideways at Echidna, wondering if she recognised the word.

If you don't look any further afield than your own work place, the teacher went on, *and can do all your shopping and other business by bus, that's probably all you need, but in this country, it's normal to get your driving license when you turn eighteen*. But he was apparently thirty now, and though from the normal point of view it was only natural to have a license by now, and a girlfriend, and to take trips and change jobs, he showed absolutely no sign of any of it, she went on. His parents had divorced when he was little and his mother had gotten custody of him, but she'd died young and all his energy seemed to have gone into making himself independent with nothing to spare for the rest. *But he's basically a good kid*, she added.

"He's scared of things, that's what. Everyone around here carries on about how this town is the best place in the world, why would you ever leave? All that. But him, he's rigid as a board. He's frozen at the age of sixteen."

Salimah didn't ask Echidna what *weirdo* meant. She would normally have asked then and there, but she felt deeply reluctant. For some reason, she had the feeling that it was a word that everyone would be very sensitive to. Not just the people she was with now, but her sons, her co-workers, the public officials who sometimes came calling, and if you weren't careful the whole town. *Weirdo* was a word that had been eating away at the supervisor since he was sixteen, it seemed to her. A kind of excitement gripped her at the thought. In her head still rang the brief words he'd muttered, *you're different*.

Suddenly it occurred to her that when she whispered to Echidna like a magic spell, *you shouldn't be here*, perhaps she had looked the way he looked then. She hadn't wanted to see Echidna pressed in there among the slabs of meat and fish—the way the supervisor had pressed himself in behind the glassed-in room at work. Freezing everything in him, there in the silence where light bounced back from the windows and nothing could approach. He had twice the ability and drive of many others, yet a few setbacks combined with the prejudice of those around him had forced him to choose to spend his days in that airless place. It was none of her business, but still Salimah couldn't bear the thought. People dismissed him as cold, but on the contrary, it sometimes seemed to her when they exchanged words that his lukewarm manner was a way of reining in an almost uncontrollable emotion. And surely, in Echidna's case too, that flatness of everything about her, from words to facial features to gestures, that impression of monotony could in fact hide a self in turmoil. She'd said she believed that the sun she saw was a special sun, hadn't she?

You're different. How often Salimah had repeated those words to herself? Now once again her lips moved, careful to remain unnoticed by her teacher and classmate, and she watched as her shadow murmured the words. "You're different." Perhaps it was her excellent pronunciation, but something now seemed to have bridged the huge gap between herself and those words. There was a magic in the words that fell from her lips on this bright afternoon. They seemed to fit her consciousness precisely. She was well aware that there was no forgiveness in this little group of sheep for someone who left the mob, wandered from the path, and chose his own way. Perhaps the word *weirdo* indicated someone excluded from the group. But she herself hadn't been born and bred in this group. *I'm different*—she said it aloud.

So they were born here and were happy to die here. Was this a boast? Or was it really a form of self-deprecation? If what they felt was indeed this mixture of scorn and anger, any sudden outlet would bring it seething out unchecked in the form of contemptuous and unjust treatment of others, thereby reinforcing for themselves the worth of their territory. And if the trigger that opened that vent was the word *different*, that word that the supervisor sent out into the world like a hero setting off on an adventure, then a *weirdo* might be a whole different kind of person, one whose fate it was to fight those who stampede along gripped by the urge to neither understand nor be understood. If this were not so, surely he wouldn't look at her the way he did. *You're different. And that's good*, he had said.

We were born of earth, that's why we're the colour of earth. Suddenly she remembered her mother telling her this when she was little. Memory after memory began to surface. Beneath a blue sky, learning to write under a great tree that sheltered her instead of a classroom roof. The first letters she had written with her finger in the sand. Letters that a man's feet had trampled. The land where she lived, her family, her friends—all taken from her. And after that, the simple prayer that she live another day to greet the sun again.

Mock me if you will, go away if you want to, but no one can take from me what I was born with, and no one will ever again take from me what I've gained—Salimah felt her temples, her forehead, cheeks, ears, her whole face burn like fire. Her ears filled with the beat of the blood that was coursing through her body like a warm spring. A sudden fierce emotion rose up in her. She glanced at Echidna beside her. *I know you, you'll be thinking all sorts of things in that clever head of yours, you'll have all sorts of things you want to say*, she told her silently.

Then her eyes turned to follow the supervisor's back as he disappeared like a little dot into the corner of her vision. Too young to be condemned by the word *weirdo*, despite all he yearned to do. She thought of her work-mates, her ex-husband, her sons. Is "getting X at Y" really all they need in life? People yearn so much for the obvious things, but they look anything but happy. They've given up on what they once had, learned to fake it, fallen silent.

I don't accept the implications of that word weirdo. *I'm different. I don't give up. Even if someone else gives up, I don't. Even if you all give up, I won't. You may force me to do the usual things, to fit in with the way people are here, but you can't twist my heart around. It doesn't matter if my talk to the class just tells the story of a completely everyday childhood, but I can't let my sons go unless I've brought home to them that they were born in a vast land where the sun shines day after day. I don't mind if they forget about their mother, but what can they hold onto unless they understand and take pride in their own birth and upbringing?*

It's for their sake—or at least for the sake of my younger son. The next day, Salimah would pack the self she had lived until now into the form of a little string-bound booklet and present it to the little boy. How much patience and effort she had put into hearing, speaking, reading, and now setting down in bound form the foreign language that for two years had been her means to living here, that language that had become her son's native tongue! *This is the language I use to give myself to him, to fight on his behalf. And in a few days, the self who has struggled all this while, with the words "for the sake*

of my children" on her lips, must die and I must live
another day. Live to see the sun, that single being that is
unchanging wherever you go. I tremble with fear at my
unknowable rebirth and its possible pain. But I will just
let this trembling self be, and talk instead to the shadow
behind me. Tell it that I swear to take in my hands that
orange colour that like a fire will melt the ice-cold weirdo.

Her little boy's classroom was close to the school
entrance. The walls were crammed with pictures and other
artworks, and paper fish dangled from the ceiling. She was
aware when she walked in of a particular smell. She couldn't
guess what it was, but it pervaded her older son's classroom
too. The smell of paper, whiteboard, writing implements,
glue, and other stationery mingled to create something that
filled the square space like a thin membrane—the smell of
children. In one corner stood the big teacher's desk. When
Salimah appeared, the young teacher rose and went to greet
her. *Thank you for coming today.* Salimah showed the teacher
her written piece and explained that this was the only way
she could be of help, and the teacher slowly turned the
pages, reading intently. After a moment's thought, she suggested they hold the talk in the library.

The teacher tidied away the projector and whiteboard,
and moved the children to the library. Among them, trailing along last in line as they came through the door, was
her son, carefully ignoring her. The library was a large
building with bookshelves along every wall. Glass windows and a skylight let the natural daylight stream in, and
in the middle of the room was a shaggy rug with cushions
and sofa where the children settled, apparently accustomed to the routine, some lying on the floor while others

jammed together onto the sofa. A particularly large armchair stood beside a stand, and here Salimah was seated while the teacher sat on the other side of the stand in an aluminium folding chair. While the children's chatter slowly died, the teacher explained that Salimah had come from Africa and that she was learning English. Then she turned to Salimah and asked her to introduce herself, and Salimah timidly opened her mouth and began to speak.

"My name is Salimah. I work in a supermarket, cutting up meat and fish and putting it in plastic trays. Do you all like meat and fish?"

Salimah pronounced the words with earnest care, giving her full attention to the way she used each familiar word. Every child was watching and listening intently to this curious visitor, though she noticed that her own little boy was looking down in apparent embarrassment. All the children now turned and whispered to each other about how they liked beef best, or had two thousand sheep at home, or loved fish and chips. The teacher now stepped in to tell them that the meat or fish they ate at home that night might have been cut up by Salimah, and the children turned admiring and friendly eyes to her. Emboldened by their gaze, Salimah looked down at the pages she had placed on the stand.

"Before I came here, I lived in Africa. This is the story of that time." Taking a deep breath, Salimah now began to read.

"Salimah"

My house was on the sand. I had a father and a mother and two younger brothers.

Every morning when the sun rose, I went with the sun to school.

Under a big tree, I wrote letters in the sand with my finger. They soon disappeared with the wind. I wrote them again.

When the sun climbed to the top of the sky, I helped my mother at home. I carried water or boiled water. When that was finished, I took my younger brothers out to play, and I played with them. We played racing and sang songs. We also danced a lot.

When the sun was about to set, I put my brothers in the bath. They cried when the soap bubbles got in their eyes.

When I was told I didn't have to go to school any more, I helped work in our field.

When the crop was almost ready to eat, fire came all over it. Fire balls fell in front of me, to my right and left, over me and under and behind me. I ran away. I was pulling my older brother by the hand and carrying the younger one. I ran and ran.

My mother ran after me. My father didn't run after me.

I grew up, and got married.

I soon had a baby boy and my life became busy. And the troubles began again.

My husband ran away. I ran away too. I was holding my baby.

My second boy was born on top of a dirty blanket.

Everyone said that he would surely not live long.

That is why we came to this big island.

I was brought up on the sand.

Also my father, my mother, my brothers.

The crop in the field was shining and ready to eat.
I decided to believe that this was all a dream I had.
A dream of the orange sun always up there in the sky.

When Salimah finished reading, the children sat in silence. The teacher frankly thought that the story was too personal to be much use for the children's projects. But it was certainly "an Africa you could never learn about from the class material." What's more, after hearing the story the children were extremely quiet, and young though she was, she had learned from experience that when children are truly surprised or moved they forget how to express themselves and say nothing, so she waited for them to slowly begin to talk again. Beads of sweat stood on Salimah's tense brow.

A clever-looking child raised her hand and looked straight at Salimah. Hadn't she been scared?

Where had her brothers gone? another child asked. Her father? Hands began to shoot up with new questions. Relieved that the children had apparently understood her English, she answered the questions slowly and carefully.

"Of course I was scared. While we were escaping, both my brothers went to heaven. My mother became lost. After my father went to put out the fire in our field, we never saw him again."

"I hate getting soap in my eyes, too. It really hurts," said a boy, rubbing his eyes with both hands and smiling. *Children are the same everywhere. If that hadn't happened, that place was a good place*, Salimah said, and as she and the boy exchanged smiles, she seemed to glimpse in his infant face the features of her own brothers. In that instant, she felt suddenly that her long wanderings were over and she had finally arrived, as if she had at last come to the pure spring water of an oasis in the desert.

You were scared, weren't you, Salimah? a girl then asked, just as she might have spoken to a friend. *Salimah, are you scared now? Are you happy now?* insisted the girl. She had a red ribbon on the end of her plait, and she was looking at the picture of the setting sun on the final page and back to Salimah, as if seeking the happy ending that a picture book should always have.

I was scared. There were so many things I didn't know when I came here, and I was scared. But I just wanted so much for my little boys to live. Salimah bit her lip a little. *When I came here, I learned to do things I couldn't do before. This is a good place, too. So I'm happy. Even though I'm alone, I'm happy.*

As she spoke, Salimah looked at her son. He looked stunned. *You were that second boy who was born on top of a blanket*, she told him silently.

You're the boy who they said couldn't live long there, and now you've grown big here.

Early one morning a few days later, the train pulled in at the town's little railway station and the boys' father stepped down from the carriage. The older boy jogged up to him, the big rucksack on his back swinging with a dull thump. The younger boy too wore a big rucksack. The still cold air of early spring clinging around her legs, Salimah stood on the platform, shoulders hunched.

She was dressed well that day. The tightly fitting jeans and sweater were cheap acrylic, but their deep blue suited her dark skin well. On her feet were brand-new boots. She had looked at them every time she passed the shop window where they were displayed. They were too good for her, she thought, but the following day she had summoned the courage to ask to see them, and their perfect fit made her so satisfied that she had them wrapped. She wasn't exactly a standout mother, but she wanted to look good to leave her children at least with an impressive final memory. When she was a child, the only time she had worn a presentable dress and shoes had been to church on Sundays and on special days. Today was a special day, too, she told herself, and it was a Sunday.

She stood on the platform, her eyes fixed on her playfully romping sons. This little train that now sat at the terminus of the single-track line would set off in half an hour and return to the city. Salimah checked the children's luggage once more. Almost all of it was school material, but it was also crammed with newly bought clothes and underwear, stationery, and books. *Don't bother bringing that heavy stuff, leave it here*, her husband said indolently. The older boy did as he was told, pulling out all the school things from his bag and handing them to his mother. The younger boy for some reason set his mouth tightly and shook his head.

"Right, we're off."

At their father's cry the two boys sprang into action and leapt on board. Motionless, cradling the school things in her arms, Salimah then glimpsed the boys beyond the carriage windows. She had noted their father's cheerful step, suggestive of a jolly expedition to the zoo or somewhere, and knew only too well that this mood would not last long.

Goodbye, children.

Despite her knowledge that letting them go wasn't sending them to their death as it had been with her own brothers, and that wherever she let them go to, here they would be safe, Salimah's heart ached fiercely. But she showed no sign of her pain, and simply whispered over and over, *Goodbye. Stay well.*

The train blew its whistle. She saw her older son wave to her through the window, and her eyes sought for her younger son. As they did so, her husband rushed panic-stricken to the train door. Bathed in morning sunlight, the train slowly began to pull out. Her husband yelled something to her from the train, but Salimah couldn't catch what it was through the grinding of the wheels. She began to run after the train as it picked up speed. The salt sea breeze was cold on her cheeks.

She didn't turn around right away. As she stood watching the train recede into the distance, a sudden premonition struck her, and slowly turning to look, she saw standing there on the edge of the platform her little boy, rucksack still on his back and a shamefaced grin on his face. The boy who had been born on a dirty blanket and predicted not to live. Now, in this land and on this morning, Salimah received him as her son once more.

D ear teacher,
I hope you are well. What have you been doing recently?

Our spring has arrived later than yours, and the yellow wattle tree is flowering in the car park by the flat. When the hairdresser downstairs came home from church on Sunday morning, he started gathering up all the dry leaves that had piled up in the garden over the winter and putting them in bags to throw away, and everyone (except the drummer) came out to help. Once the garden was cleared we all sat there drinking beer. The truckie treated us all.

Today was a sunny spring day, and when I came home from work and went out the back to hang the washing on the communal washing line, all five lines were already full. It must be that Indian woman, I was thinking, when out she came. Once a week she takes over the entire drying area with all her washed curtains, so I can't hang my washing. For this reason, I've never cared for her much, and it just depressed me when she came along with her mopey eyes to tell me how sorry she was about my baby.

I asked her why she washed the curtains every week, and then she told me they weren't curtains, they were saris. Of course, India's national dress! I realised I'd actually never seen her wearing Western clothes. She's always dressed in a sari with sandals, and in cold weather she adds a cardigan of some sort around her shoulders. But I'd never realised that saris are such big swathes of cloth without any buttons or fasteners. I asked if everyone in India wore saris, and she told me she was from Sri Lanka. I was so embarrassed, my face felt consumed in flames. I've been here almost two years, and I always assumed she was Indian. It's awful what assumptions you can make, isn't it?

She asked if I'd eaten lunch yet, and when I said no, she told me she was about to eat and invited me to join her, so I had a fish curry in her flat. I have never eaten such hot spicy food in my life! I'm so sorry about your baby, Mehra kept repeating, and when I said, No no, apparently these things are quite common, she replied firmly that it was just unbearable to think of, there was nothing more agonising, it's a nightmare that just goes on and on. We didn't go into any further details with each other, but perhaps because of the heat of the curry, we both ended up in floods of tears and sniffles. In difficult English, she told me she'd come on a tourist visa to look after her son, who is a medical student, but her visa had run out and she didn't know what to do. Do you know of anyone else in her situation? I hope there's some way to find a solution.

My work at the supermarket starts early in the morning before the buses are running, so my husband takes me. At first, he was against me doing this work, but we're not in a financial position to quibble, so now I'm working full-time. The actual work is simple but it's hard. We start at 3 A.M. Once I come back after lunch and do the housework and eat an evening meal with my husband, I'm too sleepy to do anything. A leaden sleep overwhelms me before I have a chance to start thinking about things, thank heavens.

The immigration laws have changed again this year, and my husband is only just within the age bracket for applying for permanent residency. There's not a moment to spare. So we decided to consult a lawyer, but it turns out the lawyer's fee is one hundred dollars per thirty minutes. That's why going out to work not only spares me the drummer's noise but is also financially, psychologically, and physically practical. What's more, Nakichi is now my best friend at work, and we laugh and joke together.

She's taken me back to Roslyn's English class again, and Roslyn is checking my unfinished thesis (I'm the only person to choose such an outdated theme as "The Impressionists and Orientalism," but Neil strongly encouraged me to finish it, saying I was bound to provide a different viewpoint from the overly-subjective Western approach to the topic). It makes me angry to find myself doing such a thing after all this time. I believed there was nothing left for me when my daughter died, but what you say is true: there was still writing. It's just an academic thesis that's destined for the dusty shelves, and I'm handling dry material from centuries ago, so it's no burden on my nerves. And besides, the proximity of the subject and predicate of sentences in English makes me more daring in what I write. The time when I'm writing is the only time I don't think about my daughter, and my thoughts seem at one with my physical self. But can I really think in this language? Perhaps my boldness is really only a matter of rushing straight to conclusions.

I used to despise my husband as a cold-hearted man who can immerse himself in his research and forget his own daughter, but now I understand, and I pity him. He's in thrall to the demon of research, and no matter what may happen there's no escape for him. In his heart, he may weep over his dead daughter, but he's allowed these emotions to be held to ransom by Whorf and Sapir et al. He's made his choice to become a mere hanger-on in a discipline that has almost nothing to do with real life. Watching him has convinced me I must sell my own soul to the devil of writing, argue down the thousand emotions that torment me, and hold my life together in order to serve this demon until I die.

Meanwhile, I continue to spend time at the top of the stairwell with the truckie. He's still very easily moved to tears. Just the other day we read the scene in *Charlotte's Web* where the mother blows her nose as she watches the retreating figures of the children at the fair as they set off by themselves towards the stalls and merry-go-rounds, and he blew his nose too as I read. He told me he never again wanted to experience the sight of his child leaving. When his wife left him, he said, his tiny son's back as she led him away looked unbearably small. It's hard to be parted by death, but it's also hard to be parted by life. And when it's your own child there are things you can't say about the whole thing to anyone else, things that haunt the rest of your life with pain.

But speaking of such things, I must tell you about Nakichi's recent harrowing experience of parting. She has two boys, but the older has left to be with his father. The younger boy has stayed with her. She was prepared for them both to leave. Some heartless people at work were saying all sorts of things about her behind her back—that no mother should let their child go, that her salary's the highest among us and she's chosen the money over her own children instead of resigning to follow them, and so on. Nakichi must have made this decision with an iron nerve, so I can only assume there are deep reasons for it, though I haven't asked her and I don't want to know. My feeling is that, like Mehra, she doesn't want to have these questions broached and only wants sympathy and comfort.

Before she sent her boys away, she was invited to talk about Africa as part of a project for her younger son's class at school, and she wrote a little essay for them about her home country. To be honest, the finished product itself was terribly clumsy. But you know, I've never read anything that strikes the reader more forcibly. I was astonished to realise that she could speak so strongly, despite her lack of skill. In fact, it excites me so much I can scarcely contain myself. When I read it, I found myself turning to look at her, stunned by the thought that this person might be someone really amazing. But it was just the same old face of my friend that I saw. In any case, "The Spiders" and "Francesca" are not worthy to wipe the feet of that essay of hers.

Anyway, she has let one of her sons go and is going to bring up the other boy alone. Recently I've noticed him waiting patiently by the back door when she finishes work late. That never used to happen.

You know, people around me try to comfort me by saying, "You're still young, you're sure to have another baby before long," but I can only long for her to be alive right now. I wake in the morning and see that urn of ashes, and though a new light-filled day is everywhere around me, in this world where she no longer exists light is merely another variation on the oppressive whiteness of ash. The Impressionists loved to paint bright, cheerful scenes of human life, an outdoor world of picnics and dances and cafes and fields, playing with natural colours that shift with light. For them, light was the joy of life, a palette of pleasures. But for me now, all I see in that light is the melancholy that it displaces and the gloom that lies beneath it. What on earth have I seen up until now? I could see nothing.

You know, I didn't understand anything. That's why I could so unhesitatingly write those fairy stories about life.

But now, in this little heap of ash, I see the life and death of my child, all the love I poured over her, and the pathos of losing her.

That's why I won't be writing any more fairy stories.

S.

E chidna was late for work. Aware of how punctil-
ious she was about phoning to apologise when she
was even five minutes late, Salimah felt suddenly
uneasy. As she stood at the workbench while the smooth
unvarying process of the work unfolded, Echidna's pale
face appeared from behind her. *What's happened?*
Salimah asked. *I'm pregnant*, Echidna said as she put on
her rubber gloves, in a murmur so low that Salimah could
barely catch the words.

The work proceeded on its normal course. Silently,
head bowed, Echidna carefully dismembered the meat,
put the pieces on plastic trays, and weighed them, then
covered them with plastic wrap. *Look*, Salimah told her
tenderly, *you can't do this anymore*. Echidna's mouth
moved with difficulty under her mask. *This is how it
always goes*, she murmured. *Always, always. I'm fed up.*

Echidna continued to come to work. Only Salimah and
the supervisor were aware of her pregnancy. Salimah
watched in trepidation whenever Echidna lifted heavy
pallets, but Echidna's expressionless features never
flinched as she worked. On mornings when she was feeling bad, she could barely wait for the break so that she
could rush to the toilet to vomit, and the frequency of this
filled Salimah with pity for her, but she couldn't bring

herself to tell Echidna to quit work. She'd come so far, after all. But this had never been the place for Echidna, and Salimah knew it. It had always been a mistake for her to be here.

New young students had arrived to swell the English class, and the red-haired teacher would choose two or three of the very beginners to read out the weather report in unison. Salimah sat listening to their painful drone as she worked at her writing tasks, recalling her own early experience of this stage. The teacher was now having her go over spelling again and again. Ever since she had written her piece for her younger son, she'd found that putting what was in her head into words held the greatest fulfilment for her, despite how long it took and how horribly difficult it was. It filled her with a deep satisfaction to carefully choose words, replace them with others, replace them again, and erase them, searching for those that were closest to what she was after.

Echidna, meanwhile, sat in a corner of the classroom reading a thick book that was quite incomprehensible to Salimah, and occasionally engaging in tortuous discussions with the teacher. During this time, Echidna's normally dead-fish eyes would flash and sparkle, and her gestures and expression would grow greedy as a hungry beast's. The teacher's eyes, as she sat there with Echidna, signalled to Salimah that it was clear this woman should go back to university study, and Salimah at last decided to tackle the subject of her quitting work the next day.

But the following day the supervisor announced at the morning meeting that Echidna was taking maternity leave. The news apparently came as a bolt from the blue for Echidna as well. The shock, astonishment, and embarrassment made her visibly shrink before the gathered women. That crowd of people who'd known nothing about the pregnancy of their silent and inexpressive little co-worker gazed at her now with eyes wide with wonder.

"Those are the rules, you understand," said the supervisor that evening when he bumped into Salimah unexpectedly in the college courtyard. *Personally, I hate to lose such a valuable employee, but in this case, it can't be helped. But once things have settled down again she'd be more than welcome to come back to work any time*, he added.

Meanwhile, Echidna herself showed up as usual in the classroom that day to type up her completed thesis. Suddenly she raised her head and asked the teacher, in a voice unusually loud and strong, whether colleges also had a maternity leave system.

Unlike Echidna, Salimah's days continued unchanged. She shuttled between work place and class as always, and though she sometimes talked to the son who had gone to live with his father, as time passed there was less and less they had to talk about, and she was aware of an ever-widening gulf between them. On the other hand, with the younger son who had stayed behind with her, a relationship sprang up that was almost companionable. *If it's okay with you, it's okay with me*, he would say, almost as if he saw his mother as his best friend now. This made Salimah happy, and her son's existence became a support in all she did.

Since the day they had watched the train leave the station together, this little boy stood as if he were on tiptoes to look up to her. His teacher no longer had to protect him from the bullies at school. And every week, as his little fingers turned the pages of the books he brought back from the school library, Salimah was filled with an inexpressible pride and joy. She vowed to herself to give him a good education, to send him to school until he reached adulthood.

When Echidna, her most trusted workmate and best friend, ceased to appear both at both work and at school, Salimah's heart wilted like a flower left in a vase of old water. The days, once so filled with life and cheer, now seemed empty to her, and it brought home to her with strange force that although she'd had many friends over the years, Echidna was the first whom she trusted through and through. Now once more she entered a time when she talked to the shadow behind her. Unless she did this, she felt in danger of losing sight of all she had gained, and falling into the imperatives of "You can get X at Y." Not for anything would she give over her future to the control of this sort of mindlessness, but she would have to be careful, she knew. She was surrounded by opaque certainties, and equally invisible uncertainties, and it frightened her. Almost prayerfully, she sought out her shadow and she held it tight. *You're the only one who will never leave me no matter what.*

It wasn't all that often that she had the experience of hearing her own name called.

The voice came from behind her in the supermarket produce section, just as she was putting a bunch of bananas into the trolley her son was pushing. It was a very familiar voice, and she immediately knew who it was without turning around. Her son, however, turned with open curiosity to gaze at the speaker.

I haven't seen you for ages, how've you been? Coming towards them was Olive from the old English class, her swaying body still bigger these days. Her hair was now completely white. A man of similar age was beside her, smiling amiably. Olive threw out her arms and hugged Salimah warmly, then turned and gazed with earnest tenderness at the little boy beside her, hugged him too and stroked his cheek. The boy had never been touched like that by someone he didn't know, but though he flinched a little, his downturned face was beaming with pleasure.

In truth, Salimah found this ageing Italian or Greek woman rather difficult to cope with. She didn't care for Olive's nonchalant air of always being in the know about the situations of those of her sex who were twenty or thirty years her junior. Salimah also disliked the abrasive assertions of opinion that ignored the fact that Olive herself had never worked and had depended entirely on her Australian husband all these years. But perhaps because they were now outside the classroom, she was surprised by how warmly she felt for Olive suddenly. There was also the fact that Olive no longer had quite the old forcefulness; there was a new weakness there somewhere, a mutedness of movement and gesture despite the same old bearing of the experienced mother. This must be what they mean by advancing years, thought Salimah.

Quite unconcerned by the possibility of such thoughts, Olive introduced the man beside her as her husband. The big hand that rested lovingly on Olive's shoulder bore the unique print of a labourer's years of sweat and heavy work. Olive's hand, which had a similar look to it, lay gently over his. In the moment she saw those hands, Salimah suddenly realised that she had had no inkling until now of what this woman may have thought, delighted in, or resorted to for support down the years of her life in this small town in what for her was a foreign land. The man beside her looked at first glance like a typical local, but faced with Salimah, whose appearance was so unlike other people who were normally seen in these parts, there was a genuine warmth and empathy in his smile, unlike the usual twisted grins she was met with. Something in the expression of this man who had loved and cared for a foreign wife impressed Salimah.

Their conversation had begun as no more than a brief greeting, but as the questions about her present life and the tales of Olive's own life flowed they found themselves standing on and on beside the tall yellow rack of bananas. Her son waited patiently, occasionally slipping other fruit into the shopping trolley. Olive's husband listened with a perpetual smile to the women chat, making appropriate noises. When Salimah told Olive that Echidna had lost her child, was working with her at the supermarket, and was pregnant again, Olive fell suddenly silent.

"Poor kid," was all she murmured, but her eyes filled with tears. *It must have been tough on her own*, she added, then said no more. The gritty silence that followed clearly spoke of how she identified with Echidna's sorrow as her own, and cared for her like her own daughter. At this point her husband, who had been listening silently to the conversation, broke in. *I remember now that she came round once while you were away*, he said to his wife. *She was sorry she couldn't enjoy the hydrangeas with you.*

At this, Olive began to weep, heedless of the eyes of those around her. The tears swept away all trace of her normal composure, and her muted weeping brought home to Salimah anew the realisation that there was a fragile and sensitive side to this woman, that felt pain at the merest child's graze. *I can tell you've had a hard time yourself down the years*, Salimah murmured, her own hand spontaneously reaching out to press Olive's. She was surprised at her own action.

Hugging his wife's shoulders with a firm arm as he gazed warmly down at the two women, her husband smiled encouragingly. "So you're friends then."

D ear teacher,
 Thank you for inviting us to visit over the Easter holiday. I was so happy to see you again! I had no idea that you were planning to retire at the end of this year, or that you had set up your holiday house so meticulously. That was my first visit to Phillip Island since that night I went there with you and your old class. And you say Joel has ended up studying in England rather than here. That made my husband very nostalgic—he spent several years studying there himself. Thank you so much for putting us up for those three days.

Actually, my husband has since received a fellowship offer from Boston. They say they'll help with the visa, and the salary is in a whole different league from here. And besides, he really loves Boston. It sounds similar to Cambridge where Joel's studying. My husband was really enthusiastic about the idea, but I simply couldn't face the thought of going. It felt like being dragged away from my daughter. So I told him if he wanted to go, he should go on his own. I have full-time work at the supermarket and make enough to support myself, so I felt pretty self-assured. But God acts in strange ways sometimes. I realised I was pregnant just after the Easter holiday, and though the news made me happy of course, I didn't really want to accept it. I'd just gotten used to work and was on the point of getting a raise. This may sound like I'm just making excuses, but back when my husband got his postgraduate degree and planned to study overseas, I was still only halfway through my studies. Then, no sooner had I gained the English language qualification and put in my request to continue studying in this country than my husband was transferred to this little town. Whenever something is on the verge of happening or starts to go well, this sort of thing always happens.

I continued working at the supermarket until last week. It might be the white work coat we wear, but not a single person there noticed I was pregnant. Then, by sheer coincidence, the day after we turned down that offer, the lawyer contacted us saying our permanent residency had come through. My husband seemed very pleased that everything had worked out as it should. Things would be fine this time, he said, we'd have the national health insurance now, so we could bring up our child without worry. How nonchalant a man can be, having never borne a child himself! For me, any joy at the prospect of having another child is outweighed by fear and trepidation at the thought that I might once more lose the child I've gone through such pains to bear. Yesterday I went for my eighth month checkup. The ultrasound revealed that all was going well, and that it's a girl. The due date is the exact birthday of our dead daughter, and my husband declared with tears of joy that she must be our little girl's reincarnation, but I don't believe it. It's simply that God is testing us by giving us a new daughter.

The only thing I'm still going to is Roslyn's class. I don't know for how much longer, though. The bus never comes on time, and when I have to stand at the bus stop waiting, my legs quickly begin to swell and my belly feels heavy. But it's only at this class that I can see Nakichi now. Also, Roslyn's criticism of my work keeps weighing on me.

The other day I had a discussion with her. She's

apparently read that book *Age of Iron* that I borrowed when I went to your holiday house. I've felt uncomfortable with that book all along, but it's a close weave of the best and worst of people, and I can't give up until I finish it. It feels like swallowing poison and antidote simultaneously. I've only read about a third so far, and Roslyn, who's a great reader, shrewdly noticed the book's spine peeping out of my bag in class. In our discussion, I asserted that there's always prejudice, the world is set up to be unjust, and Roslyn began, like a good teacher, by agreeing with her student, but then she went on to say that it's possible to change this, and even a lone individual can choose to act to bring about that change. Nothing happens without that, she said. Only we ourselves, each individual, can change the way we think, and the same goes for nations.

I think she's a bit like the old woman who's the protagonist in this book. Unsparing, a fine intellect, and a deep compassion hidden beneath it. But she struck me then as just too perfect somehow. She's pristine, I swear it. What she says is backed up by both intellect and experience, and she's right of course. I know that. Yet for a moment, I was repelled by the fact that she's white, that she's a native English speaker, an embodiment of the majority, and I suddenly took exception to that surname of hers, McDonald. I must be pretty bitter and twisted. But am I really just jaundiced about the world? I tell myself I must be more robust, sort myself out. At times like this I feel ridiculously like shouting that I hate the English language. Maybe it's because I had that "Natalie McKenzie" experience. McKenzie, McDonald, McNeil, McCosh, McKinley, McKinnon, McArthur—there's no end to them, and though I'm quick to forget all I owe to the Mac's of this town, I can't forget the insults I've received from them. Oh, what a stupid, warped bundle of prejudice I am! Or perhaps this is how the human heart turns sour, by being powerless to resist the forces that twist and distort it.

The truckie is away living in Brisbane for a while, and I haven't seen him for two months. Now that he's gone, the drumming next door goes on from morning to night. He told me his ex-wife is in hospital, and he's gone to live with his son while she's away. He just loses out every time. He explained the riddle of his tattoos a little, but I can hardly believe it. How can you tattoo someone with the jail's Bible? The truckie gave a great laugh when he saw my bewildered face, and declared, That goes to show what a wonderful book it is.

As for Paola, she can now go out shopping without her husband in tow she tells me, and on fine days, she gets the urge to do the washing or feels like she might go out and do some gardening, and sometimes she even does. Her symptoms fluctuate, but she's improving by the day. She tried going back to her home in Italy, but after thirty years away, it felt too different and she couldn't take it. Her relatives had grown old and no one looked the same any more, and from their point of view, her behaviour and way of thinking was just too Aussie, and she complained that she felt lonely and left out there. She's determined to look after the baby when it's born. She insists she wants to help me do the things she couldn't do, that I should go back to university, go out even just once a week and breathe the fresh air. But my husband refuses to let the baby be left in the care of someone who's mentally unstable. What would you do if there's another accident? he says.

Right now, Paola and her husband Jonathan are painting the walls of what used to be their daughter's bedroom. They've apparently bought a new baby cot and she's made a canopy for it on her sewing machine. I was amazed when I heard this, but when I objected to Jonathon that she shouldn't have gone to such trouble he glanced back to where Paola sat, painting away and utterly absorbed. *What sort of person would you say she is?* he asked me. It made me suddenly pause and think. I'd always assumed she was a strongly individualistic type, but now that the question was put to me, she struck me suddenly as much more insubstantial. *She seems to me like a model wife and mother*, I found myself saying.

She's domestic through and through, he replied, *she was born to be a mother, she lives through being needed and helping others. You might have heard*, he went on, *that our eldest son is married and living in Cairns, but he's too afraid of what his wife would say to ever come back and visit us. And our progressive daughter is working in Sydney and apparently can't stand her mother's bovine existence, so she wants nothing to do with marriage. As for our youngest, he hates this country town and has gone to live in Hong Kong. Please don't take away this new lease on life for her*, he ended imploringly.

I wake each morning with a painful back from the weight of my belly. I can no longer sleep on my back or tie my own shoelaces. There's so much I need to do to prepare for the birth, but my head is filled with nothing but thoughts of "The Impressionists and Orientalism" and the fourth rewrite of "Francesca." The writing demon has me in his grip to the bitter end.

You will have retired from work by the time you read this letter. Have a wonderful post-retirement life!

S.

PS: Mehra has suddenly disappeared. I still see her son around. Jim the hairdresser tells me she's gone back home to Sri Lanka.

To: All
From: Hiroyuki and Sayuri Ito
Subject: It's a girl!
14/12/2005 6:30 P.M.

It's a girl!
Dear all,
Ito (Nomura) Sayuri and Hiroyuki are delighted to announce the safe arrival of
    Nozomi Hope Ito
Born on 14th December, 2005. 6 lb 12 oz.
A little sister for Yume (in heaven).

Sincere thanks to Dr. Bateman, all staff at the maternity ward of AMMH, and friends who were involved.

Work that morning began with another meeting. Since Echidna had disappeared, Salimah had begun to find everything about the work grindingly monotonous. Her one respite was to steal a glance into the glass-walled supervisor's room for the great comfort of spying in one corner the figure of the supervisor. The mere glimpse of him on the phone, or looking through documents, or standing up at his desk to stretch flooded her with surprise and delight, as if she had opened the lid of a treasure chest, and dispelled the unbearably vapid hours of each day's work. But now even this was suddenly about to evaporate before her eyes.

"I've been moved to headquarters. Keep up the good work, everyone, and look after yourselves. So long."

The supervisor had been promoted to an administrative position. When she heard his brief announcement, Salimah gasped. Having learned from his cousin the English teacher that he had just completed high school qualifications, she had suspected that he was preparing himself to step off into some new world, but never had she imagined that he'd dismay her in quite this way. Suddenly he no longer seemed like a weirdo but just the same as all the others of his generation, while Salimah sensed that her budding self-respect and aspirations would mean nothing to her without him.

For several weeks after this, as soon as she got home from work around noon each day, Salimah went straight to the shower and cried. When she had first begun working, she had tasted the warmth of her own tears in this hot water, but now she could feel nothing. She stood there in the middle of the glass shower cubicle crying soundlessly until the last of the hot water had run from the tank and the shower turned cold. Once, as she stood there, she saw red blood washing down the drain with the water, and a fierce anger rose in her. How galling to be reminded that she was a woman, after all, a woman who could still bear children.

It was only when her little son spread his homework on the kitchen table that hope sprang up in her again. When she asked him to read her the books that he brought back from the library, the little boy who had once joined his brother in mocking their mother for not understanding English now proudly snuggled up close beside her every evening and read her stories full of childish hopes and dreams in his sweet high voice. At times when she was depressed, she sometimes found herself close to tears to hear him reading in such natural English, happy to please her. If it weren't for this child, she told herself, I really would be all alone in the world.

Until this moment, she hadn't had the time, the money, or the mental space to be conscious of just how tenuous it felt to be really alone. But now things were beginning to change. She had risen to head of her work group, and people were saying she may even be promoted to supervisor.

All her co-workers were fond of her because she looked after them so well. She had a stable salary plus extra bonuses. Health insurance allowed her to go to the doctor or hospital any time she needed. A part of her salary each month went automatically into a pension, and anything left over went into savings for her sons' future. She was still far from good at English, but at least she could now successfully communicate whatever was necessary. And above all, she was in a country that was at peace.

Yet why was her heart so sore? The beat of blood in her ears grew still fiercer, more insistent.

One morning, while Salimah was preparing to leave for work as usual, just sitting eating her toast and watching her sleeping son, the phone rang. She still didn't enjoy talking on the phone, and she was reluctant to pick up the receiver, but she decided that anyone who rang at this hour must clearly have some urgent business with her. No sooner was a simple "Hullo" out of her mouth than a wildly excited woman's voice poured from the receiver. The deep, rounded tones of Olive.

"She just had the baby! Just fifteen minutes ago!"

It took Salimah only a second to realise that this must be Echidna's baby, and she felt her own mouth relax into a smile. It was a girl, she learned, and they were both well. Olive reported in a choked voice that she had a fluffy head of jet-black hair.

After she hung up, Salimah wondered why Olive was so involved, but it made her happy to think that this twist of fate had somehow released some blocked air in her to flow again. She stroked her son's sleeping cheek in farewell, then leapt lightly out the door into the waiting darkness. Flooded with moonlight and cold, the crisp outside air was beautiful beyond words, and rich with the tang of the sea. A puff of wind playfully fluttered the collar of her cotton shirt and tickled her breast. In the moonlight, she sought out her shadow. One moment its elongated form was following along devotedly beside her, the next it was suddenly gone. When Salimah looked up, a large cloud had blocked the moon. Feeling a sudden release, Salimah began to run. As she ran, she thought of the transparent wings on the backs of the nymphs. *I can run anywhere,* she thought. Then the moon emerged once more, her shadow clung about her feet, and her wings were gone.

A few days later Salimah came home after work, took a shower, snatched a quick lunch, and set off with her English teacher to visit Echidna. The newborn baby lay sleeping in her mother's arms, breathing happily, as if this was her natural right. Salimah picked the child up and gazed at her. There was a faint mark from the forceps above her cheeks, but Salimah found herself impressed at how whole and complete a baby is. Her flat nose was the image of her mother's. Their teacher was still unmarried and had never before held a baby, but Salimah handed her the child, telling her she should practice for the future, and she tremulously took the tiny living bundle in her arms. Echidna smiled at the reversal of their usual roles.

"The labour pains started in the evening, but my husband wasn't home yet, so I asked Olive to take me to hospital," she told Salimah. Apparently, Olive had wasted no time in contacting Echidna after she'd run into Salimah in the supermarket. "I asked her to contact you because I knew you'd already be up at that hour," Echidna went on.

Naturally, she was well aware of Salimah's schedule. "When I said I didn't want to leave my daughter in the childcare centre, she insisted that she'd care for her." She then asked the teacher, "Can I come back to school when time allows?"

Their teacher shrugged. *It's rare for someone to want to study so soon after they'd had a baby*, she said. Echidna now turned her gaze to Salimah. "I'd like to go back to work as soon as possible, too."

No! Salimah said firmly. The other two sprang to attention in surprise. *You mustn't go back to work or to school. You must go back to uni-versity.*

The teacher stared at Salimah. Then she understood that this was no joke, and looking down at the little warm creature in her arms, she murmured as if to the baby, "That's right, you should go to uni-versity." She pronounced the word like Salimah and they all laughed, but the next moment the teacher looked solemn again and continued, "We'll all help you. It will all go well this time."

A vague smile hovered on Echidna's face, and suddenly she burst into tears. *Uni-versity, uni-versity, uni-versity*, she mumbled over and over. Then she could no longer suppress her laughter.

The bright early summer sunlight that flooded the hospital room shone on the baby's fluffy black hair, lending it a moist sheen. Suddenly everyone in the room was laughing. With her own bright laughter Salimah felt a great gust of air that had long been caught in her throat come bursting forth, and was aware of something new approaching within her as she drew fresh breath.

These days, she no longer needed to collect her son from school. His good friend lived right nearby. Salimah bought her son a bike and helmet just like the other boy's. The first time he came to visit, Salimah was secretly astonished to discover that her son had a school friend to play with, but she hid her surprise as she welcomed him in, and later stole glances as they played at building tiny Lego cars and towns. She gave them a snack of orange juice and donuts which his friend consumed with delight, with a polite thank you to Salimah when he'd finished. And as he was leaving he thanked Salimah again. His good-natured blue eyes looked up at her from beneath his rainbow-colored helmet and the blond hair that stuck out from beneath it and he carefully pronounced, "Thank you for inviting me today." Salimah's son waved to his friend from beside her, and said a little wistfully, "Please come again."

"You can come to my place next time. I'll tell Mum you're coming," his friend replied easily.

And sure enough, one afternoon that weekend her son was thrilled to learn that he really had been invited round there. Salimah had never seen her son so over the moon, in fact. When she took him to the house, a pale blonde woman who was surely his friend's mother emerged from the door. "I'll look after him all this afternoon. Please come and get him in the evening," she said to Salimah gently, then invited her in for a cup of tea.

This was the first time Salimah had set foot in a local's home. Her son exclaimed over and over that the place was just like a castle, and the two boys flew out to the backyard and began bouncing up and down in turns on the trampoline, flinging out shouts of delight.

Salimah secretly felt much the same as her son. You could cook anything in this kitchen, the green lawn of the garden was like a park, sheltered by beautiful big trees and crammed with a slide, swings, and other playthings. In the living room, sofas were ranged around the TV, and a large dog lay on the oceanic expanse of thick carpet. Now a little girl had come downstairs and clung to her mother's skirts. Her mother took a juice pack from the big refrigerator, bent the straw, and gave it to her.

Dazzled by the symbols of affluence all about her, Salimah couldn't really take them in, and instead fixed her gaze on the little girl's sash, which danced about her as she danced herself. Salimah and the mother exchanged only idle chat, but Salimah had never spoken to a local except at work and school, or been addressed by one, and she found the experience nerve-wracking. She hastily drained her mug of tea and fled, but once outside she paused to look back at the house. How grand it was. What would you have to do to live in such a castle? Turning to look back once more from the entrance, her eyes carefully took in the roof, the brick walls, the garden full of begonias and petunias, the driveway with its two parked cars. Later, the scene came back to her again and again, together with her son's joyful face.

Since they lived so close, the two boys began to go to school together. The other mother was relieved and happy, too, she said, since she'd always worried about her son bicycling there alone. Any time Salimah came home late from overtime at work, the other mother would look after her son for her. On days when work finished on schedule and there was no English class, Salimah asked the little boy around to play at her house.

Her son had only ever hung around his older brother before, but now his own circle of friends was belatedly widening, and Salimah found herself automatically brought into the circle of mothers. At first, she could say no more than a timid "hullo" or "thank you," but as people spoke to her more, she grew less satisfied with these simple responses. She did her very best for the sake of her son. For him, she could do anything. *Thank you for looking after my son recently, Melissa. Tom is good at sports. Jayden studies well, doesn't he. My son really likes Riley. Thank you for inviting my son to Brendan's birthday party.* To a bystander, it might sound horribly poor English, but there was no ignoring this woman who struggled to thank them so earnestly, and who sent along to their sons' birthday parties handmade cakes with delicate icing decorations that must have taken much care to make. Until now, in fact, the negative image of Salimah as *that refugee woman who comes alone to collect her son* had hardened them against her, but these country wives were simple, unaffected folk at heart and quite straightforward; once they had taken her under their wing, like a hen with her eggs, they listened to her attentively, and their warm gaze now turned from their own children to include her son as well.

Salimah herself was completely unaware of this. She was nervously intent on simply saying the right thing to them for the sake of her son. Watching him go pedalling away to the park with his friends, she thought with admiration how good he'd become at bike riding and speaking English.

Dear teacher,
How was your Christmas?
When summer comes around this town begins to glow. During the day, the beach is absolutely thronged with tourists there to surf, but in the evening the locals come out to cool off. The funny thing is, you can tell just by looking at them who's a tourist and who's local. From their clothes and way of talking, or just from the look of them. Even people who live close by rent a campervan by the sea for the summer and spend their nights there. Sometimes they stay on there even after the Christmas holidays are over and commute to work from the campervan, so morning and evening you see men and women in suits. The remaining adults put up tents as beach shelters and the kids play like puppies until late in the day, then the workers come back in the evening and you can hear them all outside their caravans, eating and drinking and talking together, voices raised against the sound of the surf. There's nothing special about it, but everyone seems to enjoy being with family and friends. That's how everyone spends the summer around here. The summers are incredibly short, so I guess people want to get all the pleasure they can from the sun. My family has also taken up the local habit and now we too go out every evening to cool off on the beach.

Thank you for your congratulatory phone call and flowers when my daughter was born. She has received so many blessings. It was an easy birth, and perhaps thanks to a good flow of milk, she sleeps beautifully. Her name is Nozomi, which means Hope—we gave it to her wanting her to hold on to hope in her life. Three months have sped by already, and her face has begun to have expressions. Sometimes I'm wracked with horrible guilt when I find myself comparing her to the daughter I lost, but I've finally learned to lift my spirits by finding little quirks or ways of crying that are different. When my husband comes back from work he always picks her up and hugs her.

Paola came round to help as soon as she was born. She does washing and shopping for me, and sometimes brings a big pot of soup she's made. With Nakichi and Roslyn's encouragement I'm preparing to go back to university in July for the second semester, having missed the start of first semester in February. My plan is to leave Noni (Paola's pet name for my daughter) in her care. The problem is that Paola won't take any money for this. She generously says that this is the sort of thing anyone who's had a child of their own can do, but she has no idea what a precious thing it is nevertheless. I did my very best to convince her, but she refused point-blank, saying she isn't in this for the money, but because she wants to help me, and she loves babies and housework. Both Paola and Nakichi are amazingly sensible and flexible when it comes to the outside world, but they don't seem to grasp things where they themselves are concerned. Paola's symptoms have improved a lot, and even my husband now agrees that it's probably safe to rely on her. Actually, it seems Paola's the only person he's willing to entrust with our baby.

As is the rule with mothers of babies, I'm suffering from chronic lack of sleep. A whole day will slip by while I'm busy looking after Noni, then late at night when I sit down at the desk to try and write after my husband gets back from work, before I know it I'm facedown on the keyboard fast asleep. I'm woken by the sound of Noni crying in the next room, and on the screen, there's a long incomprehensible jumble of signs and letters. It's too bad, but this is how it always goes right now. While I'm feeding her I say to her, *Your mother never learns, does she? She's ridiculously determined to do this pointless thing that won't make us a cent.* I forget all about that pact I made with the devil and tell myself I should become like a normal mother, but there's no way I can get out of the contract now. It's much the same as the way my husband has no choice but to write his thesis and pursue the kind of research that only a few people will ever understand.

Yesterday I read the final chapters of *Charlotte's Web* to the truckie. When I read the part where the spider dies and her children are born and set out on their travels, he cried twice as hard as he did before.

The story ends with some of the baby spiders staying at the farm and making friends with the pig that Charlotte had saved. When I finished reading, the truckie groaned. *Wow, women are really something!* he declared. He went on to say that women bear and raise children, and leave themselves in their children when they die, while as for men, they can't have children and when they die that's the end of it. Women go on living forever in the children who are part of them.

I think he's someone who does his learning in solitude. There can't be many men who can do this. He's almost illiterate, he's been to jail, and he no longer has a family, so he's someone who doesn't measure up to the standards of society. Yet he can express these deeply philosophical thoughts that he gained from a piece of children's literature, thoughts that any reader would be proud of.

He looked down at little sleeping Noni, who he was

cradling in his arms, and said, *Come to think of it, I guess you're a woman too, aren't you? I'm no match for you, even if you're still a tiny baby.* Something about his eyes looked old as he said that. He hasn't mentioned anything about the time he spent with his son up in Brisbane. He's usually so bright and cheerful, but since he came back he's been much more tight-lipped and silent. The drummer apparently found the new wordless glare much more intimidating than being yelled at, because he's moved out. From the way the truckie looks, I can only imagine he's experienced the final breakdown in relations with his son that he feared so much. I guess everyone has things they have to atone for as the years go by. And I guess it may be a sign of my own increasing age that I want to be the kind of person who can listen to that inaudible voice.

You know, I'm filled with affection for so much now—the people around me who are all doing their best for me; everyone, including yourself, who gives me so much advice; the little dot on the map that is this small town on the edge of the sea, now softly bathed in the last of the summer sunlight; all the work places where women busy themselves from early morning; coffee shared with friends; the rusty iron staircase outside the flat; the sound of that drum that I no longer hear; my daughter's regular, healthy breathing as she sleeps; my husband away in his office as I write; the urn of ashes that sits by the window, bathed in sunlight every morning and evening, which brings such heartbreaking sorrow to me; the manuscript sitting by my keyboard waiting to be typed up.

And I hope that someday I can repay it all—these dear people, this dear time, these dear things.

S.

It happened one evening after the English class was over.

Each fresh term saw rapid changes of students, but Salimah always remained, like the solid central trunk of a flourishing tree. The reading task that day had been the most difficult she'd faced, and it had taken her the whole class to get it done. Last was pronunciation correction and cultural understanding. When Salimah murmured disconsolately that her classwork had been rather hard, the teacher grinned. *Today's work is something high school students here do*, she explained. Salimah couldn't see why someone who had never been to high school should be given this kind of task, but the results were happier than she'd anticipated.

"Why don't you try the advancement exam?"

Those around her had been encouraging her for some time to try for a promotion to supervisor level, but Salimah had turned a deaf ear. *Still, you never know.* Salimah felt her face grow warm. *You never know*—when had she last said that? Yes, it was when her younger son was born, when those around her declared that he wouldn't live long, but Salimah refused to give up hope.

The teacher looked with amusement at Salimah standing there, struck dumb by her suggestion, and proceeded to firmly instruct her to practice from now on each day by reading aloud a page of the newspaper—not the local one but a national one—and writing a hundred-word summary of the content. She had read things in the local paper ever since she began coming to class, Salimah murmured, but she'd never read a national one. But the teacher replied brusquely that if she could read the local one, she should have no trouble with the national one.

Salimah appreciated the brusqueness. Echidna would surely help her read every last word. Olive might not understand some of the words, but her experience and pluck would help her understand the gist. But what Salimah probably needed right now was to accept herself, and run with it. It was through teaching her body how to perform her work that she had understood that action comes first and results follow. Now, with the discipline of physical work achieved, she knew—there was nothing for it but to stand on her own two feet.

That same day she went to the college shop and bought herself a national paper. Young students were clustered on the cafe terrace with plastic-lidded paper cups of coffee, chatting and laughing together. Salimah did much the same with her workmates during breaks, though that coffee came from a vending machine, and these days she found the coffee she drank there with the same old companions in the same familiar surroundings day in and day out rather insipid. Suddenly, it was this coffee with these young students that she desperately wanted to drink. She paid a fat gold coin, bought a cup, and carried it to an empty seat, where she calmly spread the newspaper before her as she sipped. The taste of what was usually a relaxed drink in break time at work now smote her tongue with a challenging bitterness, and heat enough to burn her.

As she read, the words "advancement exam" and "a house like a castle" superimposed themselves in her mind. *I must advance*, she thought. Some day she would have to climb the staircase of the advancement exam that lay in front of her, and she would climb the staircase of some house like a castle, too. The extreme bitterness of the final few sips from the bottom of her cup made her cough. Then the remaining undissolved sugar spread its sweetness through her mouth.

On the front page of the paper was news of a disaster that had happened in a foreign country she had never heard of, let alone seen or visited. It hurt her to see the photograph of a lost child squatting blankly in the mud, searching perhaps for his mother with terrified eyes. Despite the many incomprehensible words, she could understand most of the article. Suddenly raising her head, she found a man sitting across from her.

"Poor little thing." Her old supervisor had leaned over to peer at the page. She hadn't seen him for some time. His hair was cut shorter and he wore a denim shirt. Perhaps it was the lack of white work coat, but she felt a sudden flush of affection for him. Surprise and pleasure filled her.

"But why are you here?"

"They have a driving course here, and I was coming to that until just recently. In front of that building over there is where we meet for on-road training. I took the exam the other day."

And? Salimah asked hesitantly. Eyes lowered and bashful as a little boy, the supervisor drew from his wallet a driving license and handed it to her. He must have been instructed to look at the camera and smile for the photo. Salimah grinned at the funny, stiff grin on his face. She had never seen him with this expression at work.

Salimah was doubly delighted now. *Congratulations! Congratulations!* she repeated. She scurried mentally through her limited dictionary trying to find better words, but faced with his presence she could produce nothing. Struggling to add more, her words trailed away to nothing as the thought struck her that he was no longer within her reach.

Oblivious to all this, the supervisor put his license back in his wallet and turned his attention back the newspaper.

"I've got a friend who lives there. I've been trying to reach him since yesterday, but there's been no answer, and I'm pretty worried."

Salimah sighed in amazement that he should have a friend who lived in some far-off country.

"But you live in a foreign country yourself," he pointed out.

It's true, she realised, and they laughed together. It came to her then that this country was no longer just a big island or a foreign land to her, but the centre of her real life. This was no surprise to Salimah. *I came here to be able to live*, she told herself, *and to keep my sons alive. This is everything I have in this life of mine now.*

"Did something happen today?" she suddenly asked. He blushed, a hot red flush that spread over his white skin to his very ears. Faced with his fierce silence she lowered her eyes, concerned that she may have said something wrong.

Then he rose decisively to his feet. *There's something I*

want to show you. Come with me please. Salimah followed his back as he strode ahead. Horticulture students were replanting the pansy beds in the courtyard, just as they had last year. Yellow wattle blossoms, the harbinger of spring, swayed in the breeze. They left the college grounds and Salimah was led to the car park that encircled the buildings. The supervisor came to a halt in front of a normal-looking but well-cared-for silver sedan.

"This is my car."

Salimah heaved a sigh and reached out to stroke it. *It's so smooth*, she said admiringly, *and the sparkly silver is very pretty.* What would it feel like to drive a car? Limited in her life to the long narrow belt of town she could reach by foot or bus, she could only try to imagine what it would be like to drive freely beyond those confines.

"Would you like to come for a drive?"

Salimah looked up in surprise at his proposal and he hastily continued. *The sea is lovely at this time of day, or maybe you'd like to go on the highway?*

Her son was waiting at home, Salimah told him. *Well then*, he replied simply, *I'll take you to your house.*

A warm wave of emotion washed over her heart. *But he only just got his license*, she thought, and a strange happiness enfolded her. *I wonder, I wonder if perhaps this person might take me out of my small world?*

"Please take me for a drive to the sea," Salimah smiled. He opened the passenger door for her with apparent relief, then somewhat tensely circled around to the driver's side. As she was about to climb in, Salimah noticed with a sudden shock the reflected image of the orange evening sun, glowing in fiery splendour on the surface of the silvery grey car.

All but overcome by a deep sense of fulfilment and happiness, she settled herself in the passenger seat. *Put on your seat belt*, he reminded her as he started the engine. A small tear slid from Salimah's eye, but beside her, the new driver was too focused on the road ahead to notice as the car moved off.

That's okay, Salimah told herself, fixing the thought in her mind as she surreptitiously wiped the tear away with the palm of her hand. *You only have to picture in your mind where you want to go, keep your eyes focused ahead, notice everything, and strive.* Gripping the steering wheel firmly with both hands, the supervisor carefully manoeuvred the car out the car park exit. Approaching the point where he had to merge with the highway traffic, he let several speeding cars go by, then decisively stepped on the accelerator, swung onto the highway, and headed straight down towards the seaside promenade. In the rear-vision mirror, the evening sun seemed to grow smaller in a gesture of farewell to them both.

Farewell, sun. Our meetings at morning and partings at evening will go on. But this is no dream. The sun is the fire that gives me life, eternal desire and prayer, endlessly enduring hope.

The car, burnished a vermillion red, slowly picked up speed as it carried Salimah and the supervisor off into the distance towards the ocean.

Dear teacher,
Judging from the letter I received from you recently, you'll be staying in Cambridge at the moment. How are you spending the northern hemisphere's summer? Around this time of year, a lot of people around here take off for their holidays to the Queensland warmth. Winter is back again in these parts. Only the occasional person passes the flat, and today is another long day of rain mixed with sleet. I end up being alone in this flat during the day-time, and I've taken up the pen to write to you from the midst of our urgent packing for the move.

We're not going anywhere far—it's still in the same town, a little house built thirty years ago, near where my husband works. When his job changed from contract to tenured status he began to talk about moving some-where a bit nicer. If possible, somewhere with a garden where we can let Noni play without worrying. We walked around looking for a rental house, but all the houses we found were wildly more expensive than this flat, and when we looked at the huge amount we'd be paying, we found ourselves making the unexpected decision to buy instead. We've taken out a thirty-year mortgage loan, but I worry over whether we can really manage the monthly payments.

When I was cleaning the kitchen in the new place last week, some tiles fell off the splashback—just one to begin with, but they'd deteriorated so much that very soon almost all had fallen off and broken. I was so shocked I went completely blank for a moment. My husband tells me that his colleagues from work are kindly planning to give up their day off to come round and help re-tile the area. It's a simple little place, just three bedrooms and a small lounge room, but it has the bathtub I've been longing for, and the view from the windows is wonderful. Being on top of a low hill you get a clear view across the inlet, and every day we can see students out there practicing their rowing, or marine biology researchers crouching on the shore intent on some study or other. The floor still has the original carpeting, but since I'm prone to asthma, my husband and his friends plan to replace it with cork flooring this weekend. I'm very grateful.

This time last year I could never have guessed that I'd be so sad to leave this flat. We have to go before the truckie gets back from Brisbane, so before he set off last week, I said my goodbyes to him. At the end, he gave Noni a hug and said, *If you want to learn the secret of my tattoos, bring this little feller over for a visit.*

When we first came here, we only had a few bits of furniture and some clothes, but the presence of just one child has suddenly transformed it into a live-in childcare centre. Paola frowns and wants to clean things up for fear that when Noni starts walking (any day now) she'll trip over them, but it's such a small place there's nowhere to tidy them away to. Nakichi came for a visit and was surprised to find this flat is even smaller than her government housing, but when I told her we'd bought a house, she said a bit sulkily that I'm always a step ahead of her. Then her usual assurance took over, and she declared that one day soon her boy would surely be able to play in a house with a garden, too.

Yesterday I went to the university to enrol. I was sure I would have dropped off the enrolment list, but when I tried to register for the new semester, I was amazed to discover that I still had a student number. On enquiry, I learned that Neil had put me down as temporarily absent.

On the way home, I dropped in to see Paola and gave her my lecture and tutorial timetable. My husband and I had decided that we'd give her half of what we used to pay the university childcare centre for looking after Noni, but she stubbornly refused to accept it until Jonathan stepped in and convinced her to take half of that amount. (Now where would you ever find a childcare worker prepared to look after a six-month-old from nine to three for only twenty dollars?)

That evening we went walking on the beach as usual. These winter evenings, it's only the locals who walk along the cold, windswept promenade. To mark our decision to become permanent residents in this country, my husband and I scattered our daughter's ashes in the sea. The sun was just setting far out on the watery horizon. We opened the lid of the urn and held the ash on our open palms, and just for a moment it rose like smoke in the air around us, catching the colour of the setting sun, before the wind picked it up and blew it away. *Goodbye, my darling child*, I cried in my heart when it had disappeared. But it was a comfort to feel that she would now always be there in the setting sun, and though I'd said goodbye to her this orange glow, beautiful as a dream, now held a special meaning.

The first morning of the new semester, I took Noni to Paola's place. A room had been set up for her with a brand-new cot in the middle, crowded with toys, stuffed animals and a rocking horse, the freshly painted walls and carpet pink, and when Noni was set in the middle of all this, she looked like a princess. Jonathan showed us a doll wearing

a nappy and told us that Paola had been practicing changing paper nappies for days. Apparently, she's also for the
first time begun carrying an "emergency" mobile phone,
and was desperately trying to learn how to use it, dictionary and manual in hand. She said she'd always thought it
was too much trouble to read English manuals, but *since
I'm getting this money, I decided I have to be doubly careful.* I'm pretty sure this must be the first money she's ever
earned in her thirty years of living here.

Jonathan immediately asked if they could put Noni in
the baby carriage and take her for a walk. I happily agreed,
and off went my little girl, down the hill to the seaside promenade in the gorgeously frilly baby carriage that this elderly
couple has bought, which they refer to as *a toy for the old.*
I watched them until they disappeared, then set off for the
university.

For once, the bus came on time. Beyond the window
where I sat, I listened to the wind whistling by, full of the
sound of the sea so characteristic of this town, and
watched the ash-grey clouds hanging low on the horizon
as they came pressing in, a dull weight that threatened at
any moment to bring rain, and gulls stippling the branches
of the cypress trees as they came and went. So clean,
essential, and fundamentally true to nature, those hues
brought home to me with absolute clarity that I must do
what I'm truly meant to do, go where I must go. The bus
passed the supermarket where I worked for a while,
passed the vocational college, then took the highway to the
university gates where it stopped before circling the campus, returning to the highway, and finally taking me to the
far end of Glebe Street.

There I got off and walked back to the flat, thinking
about Nakichi. When I reached the flat, I dashed up the
metal staircase, repressing my impatience, hearing my

other self whispering in my ear. *I'll write, I must write, about my dear friend.* As I put the key in the door and heard the lock click open, it came to me—*her name will be Salimah*.

The horrors of war wrenched Nakichi from her mother Salimah, and she told me she'd always planned to give this name to a daughter if she had one. I vividly remember Nakichi describing to me how she reassured herself that her mother must surely still be alive somewhere, in some safe place like this. How often I too have prayed that my dead daughter was still alive! But I have learned from this precious friend and from my two daughters that after deep sorrow, one's heart will always experience a strong desire and yearning for life. I will give Nakichi this new name in my story, as someone who has been reborn in this new land, and whose life obeys this truth, like everyone who has ever decided to live in another country. And I will pour all the strength I have into the "Salimah" who now dwells inside her.

Though Salimah confronts the barriers of language and unjust prejudice and hates and resents them, she never blames others. And as a mother she stands solid as a great tree, sheltering her children from the wind and rain in the thick foliage of her love, firm and unbreaking until she has brought them up to be trees taller than her, trees that she will look up to. My Salimah will not forget pride, never ill-treat others, never bend, and never give in.

In what I am going to write I plan to put into practice all the ways of thinking and writing I've learned through this second language of English—how to throw it all away, start again from scratch, re-train. What I'm saying is, please accept what I write as a gesture of thanks to yourself. You see, you are the only person I call my teacher.

No sooner was I back in my room that day, in fact, than I couldn't resist trying to put down the first few lines of what

I'm planning. But I just couldn't get it to work in English. It has to be Japanese. And I'm afraid of writing in my own language. I'm simply terrified of writing psychologically and honestly. I've been so afraid of those emotional quagmires that lie deep inside the human heart that I have never been able to confront them directly—instead I've written in this second language of English, using it as a kind of cover to hide behind, an awkward tongue that I can only really use to gloss over surface appearances. But this time there's no hope I can do that. In fact, I feel I mustn't.

You know, I'm rather like a dog. I wear a collar called "loyalty," and the chain that's attached to it can never be severed from the native land that is my master. The day I grow so skinny and decrepit that the collar slips from my scrawny neck, the day the rusted old chain suddenly snaps, will probably be the moment I leave this world, when for better or worse I'm freed of my native land and lost to patriotism. Until that time, I will continue to dwell in the prison from which no foreign land is visible, and to serve my demon heart and soul. I have been permitted one thing to take with me from my native land, one thing through which I can extract the essence of what sustains me in life, and I will find my happiness in making from it a food to delight the demon and watching him as he gnaws. This is what my native language, this Japanese language, is for me.

My dear teacher. Thank you. For all you have done for me, for the words you've sent me, the mistakes you've corrected, all those sentence fragments that you refined and reorganised, and above all for the blessing of becoming your student when I came to this country. Until today I believed all this was simply chance, but it isn't so. I now believe that I came here to meet the people I was meant to meet, and to do what I was meant to do. If you hadn't told me to write, if you hadn't encouraged me to keep writing, I would never have written this. May this convey my gratitude to you.

I embrace you.

S.

ABOUT THE AUTHOR

Iwaki Kei was born in Osaka. After graduating from college, she went to Australia to study English and ended up staying on, working as a Japanese tutor, an office clerk, and a translator. The country has now been her home for 20 years. *Farewell, My Orange*, her debut novel, won both the Dazai Osamu Prize and the Ōe Kenzaburō Prize.